The Duchess of Angus

❖ ❖ ❖

A Novel

MARGARET BROWN KILIK

Edited and Introduced by
JENNY DAVIDSON

Essays by
CHAR MILLER AND
LAURA HERNÁNDEZ-EHRISMAN

MAVERICK PUBLISHING
TRINITY UNIVERSITY PRESS
San Antonio

Published by Maverick Publishing,
an imprint of Trinity University Press
San Antonio, Texas 78212

Copyright © 2020 by the Estate of Eugene L. Kilik

Book design by BookMatters
Cover design by Derek Thornton, Notch Design
Cover imagery courtesy of Rawpixel and Shutterstock
Map by Molly O'Halloran
Author photo courtesy of Kilik family

ISBN 978-1-59534-907-1 paperback
ISBN 978-1-59534-908-8 ebook

Trinity University Press strives to produce its books using
methods and materials in an environmentally sensitive
manner. We favor working with manufacturers that
practice sustainable management of all natural resources,
produce paper using recycled stock, and manage forests
with the best possible practices for people, biodiversity,
and sustainability. The press is a member of the Green
Press Initiative, a nonprofit program dedicated to
supporting publishers in their efforts to reduce their
impacts on endangered forests, climate change, and
forest-dependent communities.

The paper used in this publication meets the minimum
requirements of the American National Standard for
Information Sciences—Permanence of Paper for Printed
Library Materials, ANSI 39.48-1992.

CIP data on file at the Library of Congress
24   23   22   21   20 | 5   4   3   2   1

The Duchess of Angus

◆ ◆ ◆

CONTENTS

The Alamo

map area

San Antonio River

San Pedro Creek

Milam Park

Spanish Governor's Palace

San Fernando Cathedral

⑪ Mercado

MEXICAN QUARTER

FLORES ST

MAIN AVE

SAN ANTONIO, 1943

as seen through the eyes of the Duchess

1. Angus Hotel
2. Lillie's French Sandwich Shop
3. Frenchy's Black Cat Cafe
4. Kinky and Nando's Cafe
5. Joske's
6. Menger Hotel
7. Tower Life Building
8. Manhattan Cafe
9. La Tapatia
10. Saint Anthony Hotel
11. International Club
12. Orangeana at the Gunter Hotel
13. Greyhound Bus Station
14. Fort Sam Houston
15. Kelly Field

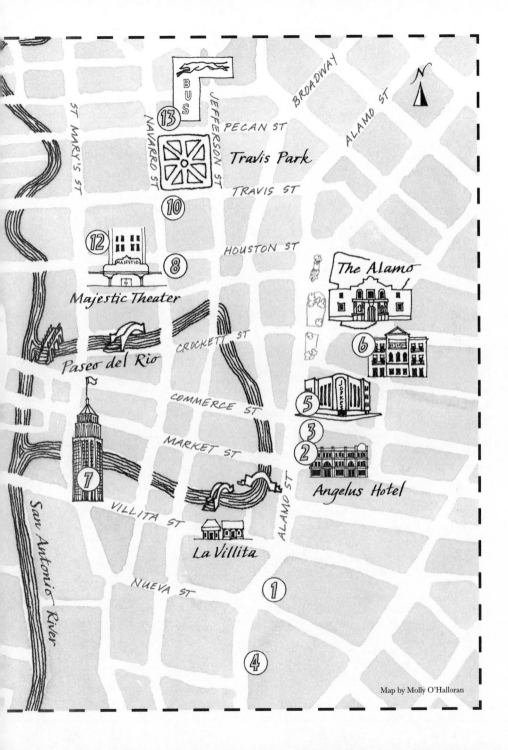

Map by Molly O'Halloran

The Discovery

Margaret Brown Kilik's
The Duchess of Angus

JENNY DAVIDSON

The manuscript of an unpublished novel whose author died many years ago automatically triggers a certain degree of pathos. When that manuscript derives from the days before word processing, even its material aspects evoke something of feeling: the uneven saturation of the letters produced by a manual typewriter with dirty type and an old ribbon; the crinkle of typing paper; the faint musty fragrance of long-stored pages. The typescript for *The Duchess of Angus* was bound in two volumes, each with a brown embossed pressboard report cover and a Duo-Tang twin-prong fastener; the paper watermark is Eaton's Corrasable Bond, a brand of correctable typing paper. Occasional errors have been corrected with eraser and pencil. But all of these details become inconsequential as soon as we encounter the arresting voice of the novel's narrator: a first-person voice inflected with some of the flat affect and disturbing candor found in the fiction of J. D. Salinger and Sylvia Plath. This is a *live* piece of writing, a novel not just of historical interest but of significant literary power and force in its own right.

The author was Margaret Brown Kilik, and she must have finished writing the novel sometime between 1955 and 1960, since the label on the cover gives Kilik's address as Readington Road, Whitehouse Station, N.J., where the Kilik family (wife Margaret, husband Gene, sons Mike and Jimmy) lived for five years at what Gene later always just called "the farm," an old wooden clapboard-style house with an apple orchard and a small flock of sheep who regularly made themselves sick eating windfalls. My mother, Caroline, married Jimmy many years afterward. I only met Margaret, my step-grandmother, once before she died in 2001, but Gene became my much-loved step-grandfather, and it was after he died in 2017 that this manuscript came into my possession.

The story of how the novel came to be remains a mystery. What steps did Kilik take to get the work published, and what led her to put it aside? There must have been correspondence that would fill in some gaps in the story of the work, but it is unlikely that the missing pieces will emerge. We are left instead with this remarkable piece of writing, and with the lost time and place and people it brings so effectively to life.

◆　◆　◆

The novel is set roughly fifteen years before it was written, in San Antonio, Texas. The work holds value for cultural historians interested in American life on the home front during World War II, in Anglo-American attitudes toward Mexican Americans in that time and place, in the lived texture of young women's experience (especially young women on the "bohemian" fringes of middle-class existence), in the cultural history of sexual relationships, and perhaps most of all in the sights and sounds and smells of a city transformed now almost beyond recognition. It is de rigueur in literary criticism to maintain a healthy skepticism about the identity of author and first-person protagonist, but in this case there is a good deal of evidence to show that Kilik drew heavily on her experience to create the novel's protagonist, Jane Davis. Jane, twenty years old and in possession of what she refers to as "unsensational good looks," has returned home in spring 1943, after four years at a small midwestern college: "Even though I posed as an intellectual and had spent a lot of time handling the more revered literature (Willa Cather, Henry James, and D. H. Lawrence at the moment)," she says, "my ideas seemed to reflect the 'even the plain girls are beautiful' attitude of *Redbook* and *American*."

Jane's patron saint is John Dos Passos, whose sway over the imaginations of American readers of the 1940s and 1950s is too often forgotten ("I spent an hour flipping listlessly back and forth between Shelley and William Dean Howells," she says at one point. "Then, in desperation, I raced madly through Dos Passos. It was no use").

Like her protagonist, Kilik returned to San Antonio after graduating from college—in her case, the University of Toledo—in 1943. She'd earned a bachelor's in English. Back home, she stayed in her mother's flophouse hotel and dated Second Lieutenant Eugene Kilik, a member of the air force who had dropped out of the University of Virginia after Pearl Harbor to enlist. Gene had met Margaret in Ohio during basic training, and was posted to San Antonio for his first assignment. Many inconsequential details in the novel are identical to the facts of Margaret's life, even down to the point that Jane Davis, like Margaret, is able to name all of the members of Samuel Johnson's Literary Club: it was a trick Gene loved and used to allude to regularly in the years after her death.

The novel vividly brings to life wartime San Antonio, including a number of important local landmarks (see Char Miller's essay "Streetwise," at the end of this volume, for more details), but the central stage is the courtyard at the Angus Hotel and Jane's room upstairs. The hotel's other residents include Jane's half-brother, Jess, a navy veteran who lost his right foot early in the war, and her mother's friend Lillie du Lac, a colorful character who at the start of the narrative has been on "a *Vogue* diet of grapes and gin and 7 Up and had lost ten pounds, according to her own calculation." Prone to making aphoristic pronouncements ("The layaway plan has broken down more social barriers than the French Revolution"), Lillie du Lac was once married to a man known as "the Colonel," who is now posted to Fort Sam Houston outside San Antonio. The Colonel's stepdaughter,

Wade Howell, works in the art department at Joske's, the same department store where Jane sells dresses in the Sportshop. Built around these characters, the novel tells a meandering yet tightly constructed story about Jane's friendship with Wade and the cryptic and unpleasant sexual encounters each girl experiences.

A deeper understanding of Margaret's life helps us to better understand the characters and the San Antonio setting she reveals in *The Duchess of Angus*. I knew the broad outlines of Margaret's early life by way of the stories Gene and their son Jim liked to tell. Since Jim predeceased his father by a few years, and Gene's death was the occasion for the manuscript passing to me, I wasn't able to ask more targeted questions about Margaret's personal life. I was able to draw on an interview Gretchen Kraus did with Gene the year before he died. The interview was for a book Kraus produced under the direction of Gene and Margaret's beloved nephew Jon Kilik, commemorating Margaret's work as a gallerist and collage artist in Soho in the 1970s and 1980s. But even with Gene and Jim's stories and the Kraus interview to draw on, I knew I needed to come to San Antonio and to talk to some of Margaret's Texas relatives.

◆　◆　◆

Della Daniels is the matriarch of Margaret's side of the family today. Married to Margaret's younger half-brother Jack, who died of complications from muscular dystrophy in 1982, Della raised three children while working at the *San Antonio Express-News*. A petite and beautifully put-together brunette in her eighties, Della now lives with her daughter (Jennifer) and son-in-law. They graciously invited me over to the house for lunch so that we could talk. I'd purchased a voice recorder with the intention of recording the interview proper, but Della began to tell some of the old stories as soon as we sat down. Eager to soak everything in, I gave up the idea of recording our conversation, whipped out a pencil and paper, and started scribbling. What I hadn't anticipated was the extent to which our conversation turned not around Margaret, who downplayed her creative talents and deflected attention from her achievements, but around her mother, Agnes, a woman whose personality and unusual choices profoundly affected all three of her children. Lightly fictionalized portrayals of Agnes and the hotel she ran in San Antonio during World War II are central to Margaret's novel, and what I learned during the conversation with Della and her family helped me to answer one of the central questions in my mind: how did Agnes, and by extension her fictional counterpart, end up running hotels of the "flophouse" description?

As a young woman born into a farming family of Swedish descent in Stamford, Texas, Agnes Olson saw clearly that West Texas held nothing for her. "I wasn't going to be a slave for those farmhands," she regularly said in later years. She was the eldest of six siblings; she had two sisters, Martha and Lala, and brothers who later settled in Philadelphia (Bill) and Fort Worth (Herman). Chicago was where Agnes went to reinvent herself. She made a living working in the then-ubiquitous tearooms and married a man who was a waiter at a famous hotel; his name was Charlie Brown. Margaret was born on August 19, 1921, and Charlie was killed soon afterward in a car accident. His family had some money (Gene said they owned a furniture store in Ohio), and Margaret spent most of her childhood living with either her father's family or extended family in Texas; her paternal grandparents would later fund her undergraduate degree at the University of Toledo.

While Margaret was living with other relatives, Agnes was leading an interesting, somewhat rackety life, whose exact details are lost to history. Gene described Agnes as "the strangest woman you might ever meet" and said that during Margaret's childhood, Agnes "wandered around the country doing the best she could, mainly opening these flophouses wherever she might be." He added, "Margaret would stay with her for a little while. Then, all of a sudden, her mother would say goodbye and leave Margaret with some relative or friend. Margaret would go to the public school that was available wherever she was. From public school to public school, she got the feeling that school was the only thing that tied her together. She was interested in studying, but very modest."[1]

In the late 1920s Agnes married her second husband, Paul Daniels, who worked with the rodeo in Chicago, and their sons Jack and Jimmy were born in 1930 and 1931 respectively. Paul left the family early on, and Agnes divorced him. The pattern Agnes had established with Margaret was then repeated with the younger kids; Agnes dropped Jack off with cousins in Stamford, for instance, and left him to be raised by them. When she came back years later to pick him up, he hid under the stairs. He didn't want a stranger to take him from his family.

Agnes continued to run flophouses throughout the 1930s, including at least one in Chicago, but what seems to have precipitated her return to Texas was an incident in which Jack and Jimmy found a bullet on the streetcar tracks. A police officer picked the boys up and brought them home, making threats about what would happen if Agnes continued to let them run wild, and she decided to move to downtown San Antonio. She ran a series of small hotels in the years that followed, so many that it is hard for anyone to remember exactly what they were called and where they were located. There was usually a small restaurant on site; Agnes was a good cook, known especially for her dinner rolls and macaroni and cheese, and by the time he was eleven or twelve, Jack was working in one of these eateries as a busboy.

The boarders—all men—were often waiters, mechanics, or railroad workers. Agnes never rented to women. In *The Duchess of Angus*, Lillie du Lac says that Jane's mother "doesn't like renting to women. It cheapens a place she always says." Lillie du Lac is undoubtedly based on Agnes's cousin Emma, who lived in San Antonio and ran another flophouse (the family seems to have used the term in the spirit of description rather than disparagement) on Quincy, with a small restaurant where young women from Joske's department store ate lunch.

In *The Duchess of Angus*, if the character of Jane's mother is clearly based on Agnes, and the character Lillie du Lac on Emma, what about Jess? He's Jane's older half-brother, while

Margaret's real-life half-brothers were nine or ten years younger. Jess does seem to combine features of both Jack and Jimmy. Jimmy Daniels ran away to join the rodeo at age fifteen, which is part of Jess's backstory. Jack served in the navy and came back from Korea in 1950 with a disability; his situation can be considered loosely analogous to Jess's return from a stint in the navy with an amputated foot. Jack went to college on the G.I. Bill, but he had trouble using his hands when the temperature was cold, and this led to a diagnosis of muscular dystrophy. There had been an episode aboard ship involving serious chemical exposure, and the paperwork filed at the time was ultimately detailed enough to qualify Jack for full disability, but Jack's health issues meant that money was tight. Life was hard, too, for Jimmy and his family (he had three sons, Jack, Jimmy, and David), who lived in a shack in Missouri where they had to pump water from a well by hand.

Money was always short for Agnes and her children, more so than the portrait of family life in Margaret's novel suggests. Gene's retrospective description, in the third person, of his and Margaret's initial meeting in San Antonio after Margaret returned there after college offers evidence of this. At the time, Margaret was staying with her mother and working at Joske's, just as Jane does in the novel. Gene, after graduating from basic training, had spent a short leave at his parents' house in New Jersey, then in April 1944 took the train to his posting at Randolph Field outside San Antonio. He met up with Margaret as soon as he could, recalling:

It was at a large house on North Main [Avenue]. He walked up the steps, and she was sitting on the porch. She introduced him to her young brother [Jack], who couldn't have been more than twelve or thirteen. She said that they no longer lived in that house, but [she] had come to meet him because that was what they had made up [and she didn't have a way of contacting him]. She told him that San Antonio was an interesting city and if he wanted to look around, she would try to be his guide. He asked if she was hungry, and she nodded sort of. Years later he found out that she and her brother had had nothing to eat but some dry crackers for the last two days. But she didn't let on during their walk through the city that the only thing on her mind was the hope that he'd ask her if she'd like [to get] something to eat.

As Gene told the story in his interview with Kraus, they met only a few times in San Antonio before he was posted to Baton Rouge to work as a flight instructor. On an impulse, he put in a call to Margaret, who had since moved north, and asked her if she would like to get married: "She was teaching in Pontiac, Michigan, which was gloomy. So, she thought she'd be better off with me. She said yes. She got on a bus with the idea of us getting married. We had only met maybe three or four times. We got married and our marriage lasted nearly sixty years, until she died."[2]

Margaret and Gene both loved San Antonio, and they remained especially close with Jack and his wife and children. Margaret's Texas visits brought unwonted glamour, and her

THE DISCOVERY   ◆   11

nephew Tim has a vivid memory of her turning up outside the Daniels house driving a black convertible Mustang and looking like a movie star. Gene's brother's son Jon remembers wondering on Christmas visits to Gene and Margaret's eighteenth-century farmhouse in New Providence, New Jersey, how this woman who looked like Grace Kelly had ever ended up in their family.

Margaret was a shy and private person, more comfortable promoting the work of other artists than her own. Strongly affected by the death of her older son Michael following a car accident in his mid-thirties, she lived a quiet life in New York and New Jersey in the years that followed. She died of lung cancer in a New Jersey hospital on September 20, 2001, a month after her eightieth birthday. Gene recalled the powerfully sad aspect of being in one's private world of loss during the days immediately following September 11, 2001, when the attention of everyone in the region was fixated on the national tragedy that had taken place just a few miles away.

◆   ◆   ◆

The juxtaposition of one's personal life with international conflict is a persistent undercurrent in *The Duchess of Angus*. World War II serves as a background, against which the moments of Jane's life—and the details of war itself—shine as both all-important and inconsequential. In this passage, which effectively places the events of the story in April and May 1943, Jane reports: "The *San Antonio Light* was black with war news. There was a victory in North Africa. Rommel had been flushed out and had slunk back to Germany. But of course this was what we had expected all along. It was simply a question of time." Jane tosses the papers aside. "Newspapers irritated me," she adds. "Their very dailiness and indiscriminating detail was as senseless as life itself, if not taken in hand."

Living in a room at her mother's hotel, Jane is torn between her desire to be indolent and a strong wish that something meaningful should happen in her life. Reluctantly she takes a sales job at the local department store: "I was exhausted from my years of floundering about in academic muck, and I wanted nothing but to float in my lush vacuum. Of course, I would have preferred to loll away the days vaguely reading or walking about through the twisting streets and along the river and perhaps coming to life for a few hours at night. But the thought of my mother working while I wallowed in indolence was more of a disturbance to my contentment than taking a job." In the meantime she passively acquiesces to dates with young military men, takes a few English classes, and drinks a lot of beer.

When a young man on a date with Jane makes a callow remark about her Joske's acquaintance Wade Howell, Jane defends Wade with a pronouncement at that point more wishful than true: "Wade Howell happens to be a very dear friend of mine." Then the girls begin to eat lunch together in the Fountain Room at Joske's, supplementing their sandwiches with milkshakes they order from a cowgirl who gets them "from the faucets in the nose of a Black Angus steer." It is the dynamic of the girls' friendship that Wade leads and Jane follows: "I was doomed because of a passive nature and an overactive sense of the dramatic to let myself be dragged about by anyone who appealed to my imagination," she pronounces.

Although well-written and engaging, *The Duchess of Angus* has its flaws. Jane tends to cast people outside her immediate circle—particularly Mexican American people—as types rather than as individuals, with few exceptions, and Kilik doesn't grant much autonomy to these characters along the way. There is the "monstrous" Mexican woman who sells Wade and Jane confetti eggs, the bucktoothed Mexican hostess at the Fountain Room, a "filthy little Mexican" child sucking on grape candy on the bus. Laura Hernández-Ehrisman's essay, "Beyond Adobe Walls," at the end of this volume offers some context for Anglo-American attitudes toward Mexican Americans during the World War II setting and when the novel was written.

The casually dismissive language about other minorities is also disturbing. At one point early on, Jane says that "for someone who didn't want to be stared at, Wade Howell was as conspicuous as a blue-eyed Chinaman, to use one of Jess's expressions." Shortly afterward, we learn that Wade has "eyes like a Hindu, dark and spilling out in shadows all over her face; not the sharp little marbles of the Orientals that remain so tightly confined to their orbits." The ethnic stereotyping falls into clear and unpleasant categories; then, too, there is the "little retarded daughter" who emerges from a taxi with Sergeant McCane and his "homely" wife.

This kind of language will mar the book for many readers,

and I don't want to minimize its presence. The novel is, in some ways, a time capsule: it features discriminatory ways of thinking and speaking about minorities and disabled people that were common at one time, but it also reveals key aspects of life for certain young women in wartime America, as well as a portrait of a San Antonio that is now passing out of memory.

One of the novel's great pleasures is the detail in which it captures a cityscape of exteriors and interiors now mostly lost to the passage of time. The girls freshen up in the ladies' lounge at the Saint Anthony Hotel, whose mirrored door features "flimsy lined drawings of languorous mermaids floating among seaweed that looked curiously like cacti." Jane watches Wade strip off her dress, sponge down her body, and shampoo and dry her hair, and then they are off on their escapade: "It was the first time I experienced the curious wave of discontent that I was to come to know so well. The feeling always soared higher and dipped lower when I was in close quarters with this girl. At first I thought it was my own restlessness and boredom with playing second. Not until much later did I realize that I was experiencing the humiliating sensation of feeling unwanted. Wade Howell wanted desperately to be alone with her own precious body."

References to San Antonio's iconic river appear throughout the text, and the waterway serves as a backdrop at times to the sexual violence that is an ever-present threat in the novel: Jess calls Jane "the Duchess" because she carries herself as though she is wholly above and apart from the rest of her family and friends, but she remains vulnerable to all sorts of assaults and encroachments. On her way home alone after a date one evening, when she goes down the stairs to the river she is assaulted by a military man. She bites him, hard, and saves herself from being pushed into the river. At home at the Angus Hotel she accounts for the stain on her dress—her assailant's blood—by telling everyone she had a nosebleed.

Aside from depicting the atmosphere of San Antonio during the 1940s, Kilik conveys the atmosphere of the hotel powerfully and evocatively. Individual characters and their motivations, however, remain somewhat cryptic. Why doesn't Jane tell anyone she's been assaulted? What drives her mother to start one flophouse after another, moving from town to town and living outside the ordinary bounds of middle-class life? Jane is in love not with a man or even with the idea of a man so much as with the appeal of this "rambling shambling life," and the novel's strongest affective charge lies in its depiction of the seedy romantic pull of flophouse living: the way the roaches go after the sweet-smelling lotions stockpiled by the professional beauty operator; the century plant and huisache tree in the back courtyard, where Jess sleeps when weather permits.

Wade's pull on Jane threatens Jane's cherished freedom, embodied partly in her free ranging about town but also in her immersion in a set of literary texts that could hardly be more alien to the environment in which she finds herself: "I pulled out a copy of John Stuart Mill as though to tuck that erratic girl [Wade] between the precise pages of utilitarianism and let her be devoured by reason. I did not need her. I did not thoroughly

like her. She didn't bore me, that was true, but the aimless escapades sapped my strength. And above all, there was the burden
of gratitude. There was bound to be a forfeit."

The grip Wade has on Jane's life only tightens, though. It's in
a conversation with Wade and her mother "at the Orangeana,
where the tropical drinks taste like bubble bath," that Jane first
hears Wade's mother explicitly suggest that Wade should move
in with Jane at the hotel. Jane says she'll have to check with her
mother: "I could just imagine my mother's reaction. She liked
to do business with complete strangers fresh off the street. The
shorter the stay, the better." But Wade Howell's advent is nigh.
She arrives with a great many belongings in two taxis, and moves
into Jane's room. The girls talk together in their room at night.
Wade has insomnia and is afraid of being in the dark by herself.
She tells Jane that when she has cramps, the Colonel comes in
and rubs her back, and that it's because her mother saw him
coming out of her room one night that she became so anxious to
get her daughter out of the house.

The Colonel visits Wade late at night at the hotel while Jane
has exiled herself to the balcony, and when she returns to the
room it no longer smells of fresh paint: "In its place was a new
smell, new at least to my room. I had changed enough dirty
linen at the Angus to recognize the inimitable odor of love."
The euphemisms of this period of American writing were clearly
not only dictated by publishers; authors brought their own deco-
rum to the page. Prompted by this intimate view of Wade's sex
life (Wade will tell Jane later that her mother doesn't know she

and the Colonel have "been doing it for years"), Jane sets out to have sex herself, asking for a two-hour lunch break from work to make sure she has time for the projected encounter. The date doesn't go well, though, and she begins "to wonder whether two hours would be long enough." The man she's targeted ultimately resists her attempts at seduction on the grounds that "some guy is going to want to marry you" ("It's a helluva time to start a classification system," Jane thinks).

The novel's denouement is oblique. At the book's close, the big thermometer on the Dairy Maid sign reads 101 and Jane, battling a severe hangover, decides that it's "high time to enter a new stage":

> With my passion for cataloguing, I began dividing myself into periods. First, a poor but bright little half orphan shuffled about among unappreciative relatives. Next, a serious half-grown Jane Davis slipping between the pages of her books to escape the inevitable. And finally a Jane Davis turned inside out...completely absorbed by the emotion of the moment. Was there a Jane Davis capable of permanent attachments? I wondered. But I was not at all certain that I was ready to enter this next stage.

Wade, unable to make a date with a soldier, encourages Jane go instead. The date is with a lieutenant, at the Alamo for a sightseeing tour. He is a young man, unmarried, a flight instructor at Randolph and thus unlikely to suffer injury or death during the war. On the novel's final page, we leave Jane running to meet the lieutenant, then slowing down, "realizing I had a whole day in the sun, and that at night a cool breeze would blow in through my window."

◆   ◆   ◆

Editor's note: At least part of the appeal of discovering an unpublished manuscript like this one derives from getting to experience firsthand its idiosyncrasies: the misspellings, oddities of punctuation, and quirks of grammar that have not yet been eliminated by the normalizing work of a copyeditor. I soon realized, however, that in order to produce a true reader's edition I would need to correct errors of various kinds. My guideline in editing this text has been to stick as closely as possible to the words that Margaret Brown Kilik wrote, making small changes only to ease the reader's passage through the sentence or paragraph.

Kilik's use of commas was especially scattershot, and I have frequently repunctuated for clarity. That said, I hope the text retains the original feeling of comma use being relatively light; it's part of the flat affect of Jane Davis's narration.

Margaret Brown Kilik's original "Duchess of Angus" manuscript, and her scripts for two unpublished plays that came into my possession with the novel, will be deposited in the Special Collections and Archives at Trinity University's Coates Library in San Antonio.

The Duchess of Angus

MARGARET BROWN KILIK

PART I

There are no flies in San Antone.

LILLIE DU LAC

◆ ONE ◆

"Jane Davis!"

At first I thought it was my own voice echoing through the corridors of the post office. I had spent Sunday afternoon answering long-neglected letters. After all, I couldn't just sit around and wait for Monday. But perhaps it would have been more rewarding to be gracefully indolent. The chore, performed with little interest and a guilty conscience, had left me restless and dissatisfied. I could very well be talking to myself. I rushed out through the swinging doors.

"Jane Davis!"

I looked down into the dark and steaming streets. There certainly couldn't be an echo on the corner of Houston and Alamo.

"I thought it was you."

Even then I didn't recognize the thin voice, but now that it was closer, I realized that the frail sound belonged to a man. Reluctantly I drew away from the privacy of the city night and turned toward my pursuer.

"Imagine meeting you here," he said.

Imagine meeting you any place, I thought.

I knew his name was Bob. That wasn't hard. Almost all the boys at the college I had gone to were Bob, with a few Bills. Just as the girls were all Suzannes or Carolyns. The last name was harder, but over the course of a dull evening that gave me plenty of time to think, I stumbled on it without asking.

"Corporal Robert Parker, USA, 26 301 564, Fort Sam Houston, San Antonio, Texas," he wrote on half of a paper napkin in exchange for "Jane Davis, Angus Hotel, 310-12-14 South Alamo, San Antonio, Texas" on the other half.

We were having hamburgers and coffee at the Manhattan Cafe, of all places. There were dim little tamale and beer shacks tucked away among the winding streets that were very much to my liking, but Corporal Parker chose to play it safe and treat his date at a spot that had nothing to offer but sanitation. Well, that was all right with me. At least it would shorten the evening.

God, I thought, how I've been squandering time!

But the night was notable in a way. After it, I was determined to shed some of my passivity and to set up a more effective defense against human slugs—those clinging little worms that are always on the underside of the leaf. This resolution was the result of one screamingly shallow remark Bob made rather than the nerve-shattering drip of monotony.

From the post office steps, I had pointed out the Alamo, a clean hard gem in the swerving mass of neon and chrome that discolored the night. No amount of trifling could take away the immediate feeling of life and death that hovered over the city.

It's alive with subtle sensations, I thought as we walked along the river, trying to ignore the murmur of love that seeped out from behind thick bushes and stone benches.

Suddenly we came to a bridge, and Corporal Parker leaped for a conversational refuge. Noting the soldiers looking down from the street, he said, "It's a crime the girls back home in Sandusky aren't having the fun—they're the ones who deserve it."

I was furious. Senselessly furious. At that time I had not yet learned to bone up on the answers in anticipation of the questions. I lacked the presence of mind to retort, and it was useless to depend upon the depth of my emotions to see me through, for like domestic champagne, they never quite bubbled up to their potential but were more often lost in the yellow liquid. I groped about in my silent prison while the moment passed.

"Take that girl out at the post."

Even then I sensed what was ahead. Of course, I said nothing.

"She's the daughter of a colonel or something," he went on foolishly.

Or something, indeed! The lumbering nonchalant.

"But let me tell you, she's nuts...a real goon."

And I waited.

"Her name's Wade Howell."

I felt that coming. The fact that I said nothing to defend Wade Howell is hardly worth mentioning. It was not in my nature to stick my neck out. What was surprising was my deep personal outrage. It was as though someone were trampling on my shadow. Or perhaps I was the shadow.

"A lot of fellows have asked her for dates, but nothing doing."

"Did you?" And I went down in the pool of yellow slime.

"Sure—just to see...you know how it is."

I made a point of not knowing how it was in the clammy little world of Sandusky Bob, but apparently my silent shout for help came through as a clanging bell to bolster his ego.

"I didn't mean—"

He thought I was jealous. He thought I was all the girls back in Sandusky being jealous.

"Anyway, she got engaged."

And the collective face of the Eighth Army, or was it the Fourth, was saved.

But Corporal Parker kept adding ketchup and relish.

"The poor guy. He doesn't know what he's in for."

At that point I might have dismissed Bob Parker as a slight lisp and a nasty little mind and held hands with him by the river. But there was that nagging little prick of conceit that irritated my pride.

I walked quickly toward the stairway that led up to the street. It was wide and cool and smelled of dampness. I enjoyed standing there waiting for the corporal to catch my mood. As he touched my hand, even the tiger lilies drooped their heads and backed toward the wall. Then I turned on him.

"Wade Howell happens to be a very dear friend of mine."

I ran up the stairs, slipped across the street, and came down on the other side of the river. I was alone beside a waterfall that spilled out of an ugly face in the wall. I was dizzy with the gentle fragrance of the night.

I caught my breath. What I had said was not altogether a lie. For almost a month now, the image of Wade Howell had been hovering within my range of vision until that very morning when it had come into focus.

◆   ◆   ◆

We had finished a late Sunday breakfast in the little courtyard behind my mother's hotel. Everything was perfect: Lillie du Lac's omelet with chili, my mother's whole wheat rolls, the starched linen cloth, the bowl of figs, and of course the coffee. Jess had hobbled back to the cot, and I noticed an unusual interest in the way he looked at the newspaper. His gentle irony seemed to be overshadowed by a deeply personal revelation. But what in the world would interest him on the front page of the society section? This mild little intrigue fascinated me.

All at once, I was overcome by one of those rare moments of intoxicating contentment. I realized I was twenty years old and had a life to live. Beyond all else, it seemed imperative to prolong that moment, that feeling.

I looked first at my mother and then at her friend and business partner, Lillie du Lac. My mother had taken off her jacket and hat when she came from church, but she was still wearing her crisp piqué blouse. With her white hair and red belt, she looked smart to a degree quite beyond her own efforts. Lillie du Lac, on the other hand, was done up more elaborately in black jersey with hints of pale pink satin. I liked her better in the white uniforms she wore all week while she worked in her sandwich shop.

The dark hair and big face on top of all that black make her more frightening than handsome, I thought.

I kept turning from one to the other as though the intensity of my gaze could freeze them into immobility. What blind observer circulated the rumor that heat makes for laziness? My mother and Lillie du Lac certainly disproved this observation. A half century of activity, sometimes feverish, sometimes foolish, but usually interesting and always conducted in a warm climate, prevented them from remaining in one spot a moment beyond what they considered necessary or amusing. My mother and her good friend were different in many ways, but in their respect for time and their realization that it took some fancy manipulating in order to be able to enjoy the daily minutiae, they were alike. Indolence was intolerable. I knew that now the food had been eaten and the conversation had lagged they would clear the table and stir up a new activity.

Another wave of the same inexplicable elation shot through every part of my body. I grabbed the newspaper from the cot where Jess had carefully folded it away for possible future reference. Suddenly I realized that I had reached for the nearest tangible object, something to hang on to. Despite my exuberant feelings, I was very unsure of myself at that time.

"What a terrible picture of Wade Howell!" I said, to show I knew the girl in the big picture on the front page.

All I wanted was to arrest time for a moment, not to peel off its filmy glaze and strip it bare. Above all, I did not want to lose this new sensation which I so inaccurately describe as happiness. In other words, I was simply making conversation.

"Now why do you want to go and take my *purty* picture?" This was more a protest than a question, although Jess would be the last to admit it. Since his disability, he had made a point of not complaining. My stepbrother had lost his right foot early in the war. After months of rehabilitation in a navy hospital, he threw aside the clay ashtrays, drawing boards, and wheelchair and set out on his own.

"I got it made," he had said. "One hundred percent disability pay is all the rehabilitation I need."

His philosophy was rather novel at the time, although he seemed to be a forerunner of a generation that was to follow. He proceeded to hitchhike from one end of the country to the other with a side trip down into Mexico before finally coming home.

Lillie du Lac, as usual, made no bones about the tone of her voice. "And I suppose you've seen Wade Howell?" she said, snatching the paper from me.

Before I had a chance to answer, my mother joined the act with her own quick-change offering.

"Wade Howell can't be a girl," she said with an innocent voice and a knowing smile.

"See for yourself," Lillie said, holding up the paper. "All girl and a yard long."

At first, my mother looked at the picture with a pretense of indifference, but soon she and Lillie were pointing at and studying the figure of the dark girl in the white dress with the same argumentative interest as two men plotting a trip on a road map.

The Wade Howell I saw looked ridiculous. From my angle, her clipped head and tan face made a lonely coconut in a strangely perky palm tree. Her slim body formed a fine graceful trunk, but it was obvious the feet would never be safely rooted. Even upside down, the pouty mouth and shadowy eyes gave her the appearance of being out of her element.

"Wade Howell, the daughter of Colonel and Mrs. Rainey W. Howell, poses by an early cannon. Colonel Howell, formerly of Old Camp Brook, is now stationed at Fort Sam Houston—"

"Why do they call it 'old' Camp Brook?" I asked stupidly.

"To make the Colonel seem younger, naturally," Lillie said. "Listen to this! 'Miss Howell recently became engaged to Major Ralph Morris Jr., son of Mrs. Agnes Morris and the late Colonel Ralph Morris Sr.'"

"She's taken their name, I see." This was my mother.

"Why not?" Lillie threw up her hands. "After all he gave up for them, he should be entitled to scratch his initials on her. It probably makes for better discipline in the family."

"The Colonel isn't her father then?" I asked.

"Of course he isn't! They've been married only five years, and that girl's more than four—anyone can see that."

A silent brooding refrain, which Lillie du Lac shared with my mother, clouded the mood of the courtyard. Then Lillie went on in shrill solo.

"She was Eunice Estes before she married the Colonel. All kinds of money—and I mean literally. Pours in helter-skelter from all over the world. You might say she has it to burn. She smoked the Colonel right out with it, and when he came up for air, she had a fresh batch to dangle in his face."

♦   ♦   ♦

I had only known Lillie du Lac for a month, but it was long enough to have learned that Colonel Rainey W. Howell had been one of her husbands. And from the number of times his name cropped up in conversation, I would say that he was her favorite husband. I wished now that I had paid more attention to what had been said about him. On a weekday when I came down for early breakfast, the Colonel seemed as much a part of the morning atmosphere as the smell of coffee, the beating of batter, and Mira, the "current dizzy" (my mother's words) who was Lillie's helper, more or less, in the sandwich shop on the ground floor of the hotel. It was usually Lillie who did the talking while my mother nodded, rather bored I thought. After all, Martha had had her own two husbands, and although ordinarily she went out of her way to preserve and revere the past, as far as husbands were concerned, she buried them deeply and permanently. One of them had presumably been my father, and she may not have felt free to bandy about his masculine peculiarities in my presence. Then again, I didn't know my mother much better than I did Lillie du Lac.

♦   ♦   ♦

During the four years I had spent in a small midwestern college, my mother had come through to me in an assortment of envelopes that sailed under my door every week or so. The words were scrawled on such an exaggerated slant that they were hardly more legible than a straight line.

"They have every right to be tired," I thought, eyeing the faded postmarks, which were never duplicated.

My mother had traveled all over the country in those days, but she never came to visit me at school. Not that she wasn't interested. Far from it. She was interested in everything. But she simply couldn't stomach "those Puritans," which was her rather liberal classification for her in-laws, the faculty, and anyone else who happened into the broad sweep of her arm, or more particularly, to live above the Mason-Dixon Line.

Despite my loneliness, the Puritans, and the ghastly midwestern climate—or perhaps because of these austere conditions—I graduated cum laude. It had been a terrific strain. I really didn't think I had the mental capacity for such an achievement. The dean of women had hinted as much during an interview my freshman year. But one of the stipulations of my grandma's will had been that I maintain a high grade-point average. If I failed to do so, the money set aside for my education would have gone down the hall with the rest of Grandma's estate to the newly decorated faculty lounge. For three years this torturous battle of wits went on. It was not until my final semester that the Committee for the Appropriation of Funds realized that Grandma had amply provided for everyone. The tension relaxed, the lounge became a plush haven for tired minds, an old photograph of Grandma was blown up and placed over the fireplace, and I pressed a tiny wartime bachelor of arts to my hollow bosom. Then I took one last nostalgic look at the frozen campus and started in the direction of the latest postmark.

For three days and two nights, as the Greyhound cut a lumpy lopsided angle across the middle of the country, I made bright plans for the future, all dazzling and far away. At the time, I was satisfied to drift along in the dust and think about San Antonio, the city at the end of the line. The very name brought to mind hot lazy days and breezy romantic nights, bright stucco buildings and cool cathedrals.

Suddenly, at three o'clock in the morning, I stepped into an atmosphere of such intoxicating mildness that future plans and past memories faded away and nothing remained but a glorious realization that I was alive. My mother was there to meet me, and as we walked through the deserted streets to her hotel, I luxuriated in this sudden unshackling of the senses that was to come over me again and again.

◆　◆　◆

"I'm ready any time you old hags get tired of scratchin' around on that paper."

My rapturous mood had passed, and it made me sad to see Jess assume even a touch of hilarity when I suspected he felt otherwise.

Although his remark did not touch off the usual laughter and protest from Lillie du Lac, it did give her a chance to come up for air. And I was the first to feel her hot breath.

"Is that all you learned at college?" she asked.

"What?"

"Why, to spoil a perfectly good meal with a jerk and a

shout—and don't answer a question with another question," Lillie said, imitating what she called my "constipated expression." In the same breath, she turned to my mother.

"Martha, what were you thinking, turning her over to those primitives? A lifetime will never be enough to repair the damage."

"Lillie, you exaggerate. The worst we can say is that the whole episode was harmless."

"Harmless? Four years of straining her eyes and sitting on her ass!"

"But she does seem adaptable. And she learned to smoke and drink under their very noses."

My mother announced this happily, at the same time sniffing the smoke of my cigarette. But it was the deceit that pleased her. I knew that she detested the smoking. Mainly, however, she wanted to point out something about me that might please Lillie du Lac. It was the mother instinct coming through. I suppose if I had set fire to Chicago on my way across the country, I would have been a real heroine to these two ladies. It would be extremely poor timing to confess that I had acquired the niceties under question at fifteen-minute intervals along the route of the Greyhound bus.

"A little deception never hurt anyone," Lillie agreed.

And all was harmonious once again as she massaged the vertical grooves on her forehead (everything about her pointed upward—Gothic style). With this familiar gesture, I knew that she was leading up to something that concerned her more than my manners. Ironing out the wrinkles usually meant that she was about to shake out some old adventure and hold it up for inspection.

As for me, I was thinking not so much of Lillie du Lac's old loves as my own prospects, which, although rather misty, were far from dim. At least from my glossy point of view. Even though I posed as an intellectual and had spent a lot of time handling the more revered literature (Willa Cather, Henry James, and D. H. Lawrence at the moment), my ideas seemed to reflect the "even plain girls are beautiful" attitude of *Redbook* and *American*. In this bright clean world, there was always a shadowy line of stag millionaires waiting for me to settle down after my big fling, which never seemed to get off the ground. I had to smile myself, sometimes.

"You can laugh now," Lillie du Lac was saying, "while you're able to walk around naked in the sun, but you had better look about you and find a neat disguise so you can be gracefully unhappy when you're all burned up."

Lillie du Lac tossed the newspaper to Jess.

"Try to improve on that."

"I wouldn't touch a button."

"I'll bet!" Then she turned to me.

"So you don't think she's beautiful."

"I didn't say that."

"Oh?"

"I said, 'It's a terrible picture of Wade Howell.' There's a difference." Then, after a dramatic pause: "She's much better looking than the picture."

"How would you know?" Lillie asked in an insinuating tone.

"I see her almost every day."

If I had fallen to pieces and blown off in all directions, Lillie du Lac could not have been more surprised. The vertical lines shot upward and my mother offered her friend another cup of coffee. But the big game had played so many tricks on Lillie that her defense was almost better than her offense. She was prepared. As she always said when she got up in the morning, "Well, the masquerade is on. Where is my costume?"

Now all she said was, "Why didn't you tell me?"

"I didn't think it was important."

"You wouldn't."

Peeking over Jess's shoulder, my mother said, "I wonder how she looks in color."

That's something no one knows, I thought.

Suddenly Lillie stood up, all fight and energy. "Don't tell me you met her in Joske's."

"Yes, she works in the art department."

I knew that Lillie du Lac was more excited than she let on. Usually she took time to pause and dream up some derogatory name for the department store where I worked. "The Refrigerated General Store Down the Dusty Trail" was my favorite. As far as I knew, she had never been inside the place. She was frugal and clever, making new things out of old with the help of little offbeat button and lace shops. But Joske's came to her. At lunchtime, the saleswomen crowded into Lillie's little French Sandwich Shop like ants in a bowl of sugar. I don't know whether it was their basic black dresses or their nickel tips that annoyed her more. She called them "Joske's whores," which meant, I gathered, that they had prostituted themselves to an institution.

"She hasn't been there long," I added.

"Of course not!" She looked at my mother. "This must be Eunice's doing. You can accuse the Colonel of a lot of things, but he doesn't lack taste."

I had never heard my mother accuse the Colonel of anything.

"No. And he's not stuffy," my mother added with a gleam in her eye.

"Naturally. The two go together. You can't be stuffy and have taste."

I think it was this word *taste* that lured me into Lillie du Lac's game and eventually to the Howells. I had drawn a clear-cut notion around a rather vague term as a result of a distant relationship with a young French professor. He was a man of taste. That is, he read obscure books and listened to concertos and wrote little French poems. He was also tubercular and an alcoholic and died sweetly and gently in the pale cold winter of my sophomore year. But before that, he had let it be known that I was, as he put it, "what every young girl should be." And although I was as far from the popular notion of this ideal as I was from my own, these words often gave me comfort.

"How well do you know this girl?"

"Not very well at all, really. I showed her how to make out a sales check the first day she came to work."

I should have made more effort to know Wade Howell while I had the chance. Not merely to gain Lillie's esteem, which I certainly desired, since she seemed to me inseparable from the place I had come to love. But for my self-respect as well. I was entirely too backward and withdrawn, and if I didn't make some effort to change, I was in danger of becoming one of those wispy creatures who latch onto stray desperate attachments. Yet in my effort to overcome this despicable quality, here I was, nurturing it as well. I couldn't resist this pretentious little intrigue, the idea of endearing myself to Wade Howell. It would give me a legitimate pose before the dark shadows of the city, an excuse to follow aimless, slightly mad pursuits. Above all, I would get to know this man of taste (the word now struck me as a comforting kind of consolation when more demanding endeavors had failed) and his strange stepdaughter.

It would have been a cinch before Wade Howell was transferred to the art department. I still saw her occasionally, floating about the store in her slow and graceful way. We still exchanged smiles, but that was all. Sometimes she came to the Sportshop to get information for an ad or to leave plans for a display. If we spoke, it was always about the merchandise.

Once, while we were going over some layouts for the paper, the subject of Mrs. Smart, our former buyer, came up in connection with some rather daring playsuits she had ordered before she died. I was on the point of making a flip remark about the complicated sex life of Mrs. Smart, which was reflected in the vast range of her selections, when suddenly Wade Howell snatched up a torrid little black and white outfit for herself. I was hardly three weeks away from my midwestern campus at that time, and I was sincerely shocked that such a nice girl apparently intended to be seen in broad daylight in clothes that were neither old nor baggy. I examined her bulky white skirt and respectfully mended black cashmere and decided there was more to this girl than met the eye.

I had a feeling that Wade Howell wanted to be friends.

She's my kind of girl, I thought, and she knows it.

But a certain reserve made her hesitate to make the first move. I understood this perfectly. I was pretty much a loner myself, and was extremely cautious in my choice of companions. I preferred cat-like people with an innate intellectuality that made them capable of pulling off all kinds of fine deceits. They were the ones who were gracefully attuned to their environment. Not the fluffy wiggly people who made so many useless movements to cover up their incompetence. Of course, I could have gone a step farther and become involved with the rodents, but they didn't even bother to lick themselves clean.

She was feline all right, but there was the restlessness of the uprooted about her. I was reminded of the stories of stray cats traveling unbelievable distances and suffering unendurable hardships to find their way back to beloved homes. Wade Howell put me in mind of those lost cats.

But it was only later and from a distance that I realized she was withdrawn. At first I thought she was stupid.

I had been at Joske's only two weeks when Wade Howell arrived, as she would have it, directly from Panama. By then I had established myself as a promising, although somewhat unreliable, salesgirl. But Mrs. Smart, the buyer for sportswear, liked my unsensational good looks, so I was treated with more consideration than I deserved. Anyway, it was during the war, and Joske's, like everyone else, accepted incompetence as a patriotic duty.

It was no surprise when Mrs. Smart turned the new girl over to me rather than to her assistant buyer. If I had half tried, I could have pushed the assistant right off the floor. She was a tall boney thing with no imagination and no humor. Nothing, in fact, but seniority. However, I did not care to assert myself even that much. I was exhausted from my years of floundering about in academic muck, and I wanted nothing but to float in my lush vacuum. Of course, I would have preferred to loll away the days vaguely reading or walking about through the twisting streets and along the river and perhaps coming to life for a few hours at night. But the thought of my mother working while I wallowed in indolence was more of a disturbance to my contentment than taking a job.

For an hour or so one morning, I looked about for something that was not too demanding. I found it a block away from the hotel at Joske's department store.

I soon settled on a workable compromise for my new freedom of spirit, which was nothing more than a relaxation of any rigid rules of conduct. As a result, I enrolled in a poetry course and drank a lot of beer.

The day Wade Howell came to work, I had a terrible hangover. I had been to the drinking fountain a dozen times. It was three o'clock, and I was beginning to wonder whether I would be back to normal by closing time. I didn't mind feeling half dead on the job, but that was the night for the Romantic Poets. I certainly couldn't expect to be carried away by Keats's images with a beery head.

As I was returning from my latest trip to the drinking fountain, I felt a disturbance in the air. At first the feeling was so slight that I almost dismissed it as oversensitiveness brought on by thinking about the poets at that unlikely time and place. But when I saw Mrs. Smart charge out of her office, and our eyes met in the middle of the aisle that separated Nardis of Dallas from Cole of California, I knew that my alertness had been justified. Mrs. Smart ran her department by ear, and to work with her successfully, it was necessary to have an awareness of situation. This subtlety was completely lacking in the assistant. I possessed it in abundance. At that moment, I knew without being told that I was being called upon to witness what Mrs. Smart considered an act of deceit.

Mrs. Fox was trying to sneak past the Sportshop over to Better Dresses. She might have made it, too, if it had not been that the girl with her refused to be made inconspicuous. She was a slim dark beauty, not very tall. And she made such a big thing of walking. Just plain walking. It was as though she led a great procession of invisible but worshipping handmaidens and adoring followers. Short fat Mrs. Smart stood still and bounced. I knew what was going on in her commercial mind: this girl could wear every fantastic outfit in the place with such conviction that the customers would be magically transported to country clubs and swimming pools. The illusion could be expected to last at least as long as it took to write out a sales check.

But first Mrs. Smart would have to get the girl out of the clutches of Mrs. Fox, who was no easy mark, having been in personnel for forty years, since before she was married, and now she was a great-grandmother. A little wrinkled and stooped, but still a ball of fire.

I could not imagine what the matter was with Smarty. There she stood, black, gray, and fat, with eyes bulging and bosom heaving, but she couldn't get off the ground. The girl was clearly marked for Better Dresses. Then, with a terrible effort, Mrs. Smart pulled herself through the racks of pure linen and fine poplin to block Mrs. Fox's path.

"That girl belongs to me. Anyone can see that. She's sportswear right down to the bone." Mrs. Smart wiped her face with a sopping wet handkerchief.

"Better Dresses are crying for help," said Mrs. Fox sadly.

"Let them cry! Let them shriek! They haven't a damn rag worth selling anyway."

"There's nothing wrong over there that some new blood won't fix."

I took a quick look at the new girl, who was vaguely admiring herself in a full-length mirror.

"Hell, they're dead! Lying cold in their coffins. It's too late for blood."

"I know their sales are down, but it's a temporary thing. No one wants to dress up. It's the war making everyone so casual."

"Then let them be casual," said Smarty, making a sweeping gesture toward her sportswear. "After the war, when their stomachs are sticking out from feeding their anxiety and their butts are spread from sitting on bar stools, we'll sell them corsets."

"I like to get paid. For my money, you can run every department in the place. Smarty, this is Wade Howell."

Mrs. Fox walked away, looking stooped and very tired.

I spent the next hour trying to show the new girl how to make out a sales check. Then Mrs. Smart took over. By closing time, Wade Howell, smudged with carbon, insisted on taking a quick sponge bath in the employees' lounge while I kept the doorman from locking her in the building for the night. The new girl had not the faintest notion how to make out a sales check.

That night Mrs. Smart died of a heart attack. The next day, Wade Howell was transferred to Better Dresses. From there, she was sent to the art department, where they created the perfect job for her. She walked about the store delivering messages. That was her forte. She walked like no one else: slow, graceful, deliberate.

♦　♦　♦

Perhaps I should have gone along with Joske's neat departmental arrangement and relegated Wade Howell to an insignificant place in my life. But between the hot noonday sun and Lillie du Lac's fierce aversion to timidity, my slight backbone completely collapsed.

"You can begin by having lunch with the girl," Lillie was saying triumphantly.

"But we don't all eat at the same time."

"You don't all eat separately, I'm well aware."

It was true. Lillie's place was so packed during the lunch periods that I preferred a paper bag full of sandwiches.

"It will be a little lesson in organization," she went on dreamily. "Once you've experienced a well-ordered daily existence, anything else is unbearable."

This was a game, of course, but a serious game played for impossible stakes, where the unspoken rules were more important than the end results. Possibly because we never recognize the finish, the manner of playing, style perhaps, takes on more importance. One might say it forms our character. Lillie du Lac had always found the sport intriguing. In fact, she found it so necessary that she kept on in spite of close calls and near defeats.

"Lillie, don't you think there's a certain amount of risk in being so obvious?" my mother asked.

"Obvious! She's not bringing her here, you know."

"I should hope not."

"Not yet, anyway—and I'm not at all certain we're not playing it too discreet." She pushed her fluffy bang back from a forehead that was so high it appeared to be receding. "After all, time counts for something."

"Don't rush things," my mother said. "Right now you're enjoying a perfect relationship with an ex-husband...a cup of coffee now and then."

"All the same, you'll have to admit that the Colonel stays within shouting distance. That can only mean one thing."

"That the army needs another colonel at Fort Sam Houston."

"Nonsense, Martha. The Colonel only uses the army as a background. He's tired of being smothered in all that money—that's about the size of it. He's looking for a strong arm to pull him out from under it all."

"And you don't get up at five o'clock and beat batter for nothing."

"I've got muscle to spare."

My mother and Lillie du Lac looked at each other and smiled.

"I didn't think that you could bear to play to an empty house for long."

At one point during the Depression, my mother and Lillie du Lac had joined a medicine show, my mother brewing the medicine and Lillie acting as mistress of ceremonies. Although like most of their fortunes the incident was an accident, which if given proper perspective should have been dumped with the phony medicine, they preferred to dig it up from time to time in the lingo of old-time troopers.

"Sometimes I think, well...," Jess said, stretching out on the cot with the society section under his ratty pillow, "and then again, I just don't know."

I laughed. Jess always made me laugh and feel sad at the same time. He turned his face toward the stone wall and the sun shone on the back of his dark blond head. I had regained some of my strange exhilaration, yet I was anxious for the day to pass so that tomorrow would be closer.

◆ TWO ◆

On the escalator halfway between second and first, I congratu-
lated Wade Howell on her engagement.

"If it weren't him, it would be someone else," she said simply.
"I've had ten proposals. Three before my first period."

I thought at the time that she was bragging, but later I realized
that she was merely stating a fact that irritated her. The prospect
of marriage disgusted her, but any alternative frightened her.

In the Fountain Room, we spread out our sandwiches from
home and ordered milkshakes from a cowgirl who in turn got
them from the faucets in the nose of a Black Angus steer. Neither
the sanitary implication nor the sexual deviation seemed to disturb anyone. At the time I didn't give it a thought. I was wondering why a girl who took over the front page of the society section
on Sunday felt the pressing need to economize on Monday. As
Lillie du Lac put it, "They can buy everything else, so they think
they can buy poverty too."

Of course, I wouldn't dream of asking Wade Howell a personal
question. There was an aura of unhappiness about the girl that

made me hesitate to touch on any subject that I wasn't certain was an established topic in her conversation. It was generally known about the store that she had come from Panama.

"Did you like Panama?"

"It was nice."

"Was that your home?"

"I have no home, not really. We lived there for a time while the Colonel was stationed there."

I wished she wouldn't make it sound so dull. Wade Howell was not easy to talk to. When the conversation was left to her, it came out in scattered remarks that had little connection with one another. This gave me the impression that she was alone a good deal. Even though she certainly didn't appear uncomfortable in her surroundings. Far from it. She seemed to be one of those human chameleons who fit in anyplace. If the conversation lagged, it was because she didn't choose to talk.

"Do you like working here?"

"It suits my purpose."

And that apparently was that. My curiosity was not going to be satisfied with anything as aboveboard as an answer to a forthright question. Lacking Lillie du Lac's experience with minor intrigue, I was reduced to silently looking at the murals of "Old San Antone."

"Where are you from originally?" I despised myself for this inanity.

"No place in particular."

That, I thought, is exactly the impression she wants to create.

The beautiful stray who is waiting around every corner. There was a raffish quality about her that suggested an uncultivated indifference. Well, wasn't that what I wanted, after all? Someone who wouldn't smother me with mediocrity. Someplace where I could escape the suffocation of being pigeonholed. I thought of Bob Parker and his regional ideals, and for the second time, I plunged into this new friendship with enthusiasm.

I was no longer trembling with anger and humiliation as I had been all night and through the morning. By ten o'clock, I had become so dehydrated from twelve hours of unrelenting indignation that I had to sneak away for a coke. In the employees' lounge, I found Wade Howell taking a sponge bath. At first, I was embarrassed bursting in on anyone so naked, but she just laughed and said that she felt sticky. As I rinsed the tips of my fingers, I asked her where she usually had lunch.

"No place in particular."

"That would be the Fountain Room."

And we both laughed, soaking in the warmth of a new friendship.

Wade Howell didn't bubble with girlish enthusiasm, so at a time when a wisecracking good sport was the thing, she seemed to me wonderfully undemanding. Her conversation was rather dull, but her behavior was anything but uninspired. We had barely finished our sandwiches when she stood up.

"I can't stand being stared at any longer," she announced.

I wanted to smoke a cigarette, but I said nothing. Instead I tagged along after my new friend. The pattern was set. She would lead, and I would follow.

As we sat at the edge of the fountain fumbling for change, it occurred to me that for someone who didn't want to be stared at, Wade Howell was as conspicuous as a blue-eyed Chinaman, to use one of Jess's expressions. She was in the same slim white dress that she had worn for the newspaper picture. Only now she had tied a flimsy black scarf around her head, and her orange shoes and lipstick made all the difference. The scarf, no doubt, was a kind of dislocated veil to symbolize modesty.

"You were smart to choose white for the tropics. It's just right against the sun and shadows."

She smiled, and I knew that I had gotten through to her.

"No, this is a new dress that mother bought for the picture."

She saw that I was embarrassed, so she went on, hoping to ease the moment with a peculiar kind of fantastic sincerity.

"The white was my idea. I consider myself in a kind of semi-mourning. A preparation for death. After I'm married, I'll wear black."

I wondered what level of purgatory the trousseau would represent, but I said nothing. I did not wish to break our fragile thread of friendship.

"I have an errand to do," she said. "Would you like to come along?"

I knew I should brush through "Endymion" again in preparation for that night's class. But I was doomed because of a passive nature and an overactive sense of the dramatic to let myself be dragged about by anyone who appealed to my imagination.

As we stood before the rose window at Joske's main entrance, I saw that she had eyes like a Hindu, dark and spilling out in shadows all over her face; not the sharp little marbles of the Orientals that remain so tightly confined to their orbits. Deep and wayward. Everything else was clean-cut and confined to the surface.

We were winding our way through the crowds on Houston Street by the time I learned that our destination was the Gunter Hotel, where we were to meet Mrs. Gordon Nickerson. I had heard Lillie du Lac and my mother talk about Mrs. Nickerson, and I knew that she was chair of the Cadet Hostesses.

"You'll like her," Wade Howell said. "She does an awful lot of good."

"What else does she do?" I was hot and my feet ached. Wade Howell was a better walker than I.

Before she had a chance to answer my question, we were caught in a roadblock of soldiers. They were all shiny and clean, and I thought rather tempting, but Wade Howell was all business, so they let us through. I treasured these slightly mad little escapades. They were part of the carnival spirit of the city, which seemed on the verge of breaking into a fiesta. Even the five-and-ten-cent stores, the epitome of national conformity, took on a local flavor with their displays of turquoise and silver, Aztec pottery, and hand-tooled leather simply screaming for the open marketplace, while the fake pearls crouched back in awe. But it was the gay little Mexican girls who, smiling sweet-tempered behind the counters, set the mood. Never rude, never dull, never tired, they lent a graciousness to the city that seemed to be in secret league with the sunny atmosphere to conjure up its lighthearted spell.

◆　◆　◆

On the mezzanine of the Gunter Hotel, Mrs. Gordon Nickerson had spread herself over two plush rooms, which she called "our little workshop." But it was she who managed to dominate her surroundings. And anything else that might get in her way. She was a slickly groomed segment of our social set, and I was glad that she had found a satisfying niche. Otherwise she might have proven dangerous. Even so, I was thankful that our introduction was taking place in a bright room. I would have been terrified if I came upon that face lit up like some sinister mask against a dark background.

"This is Jane Davis. Mrs. Gordon Nickerson."

"I'm delighted you have brought me such a lovely girl. Where on earth did you find her?"

"At Joske's," Wade said. "Did you find me a room?"

"Let me see to this first." And Mrs. Gordon Nickerson began to swallow me up. She wrote my name on a card that looked like a wedding invitation.

"What is the address?"

"310-12-14 South Alamo."

She looked up, and well she might. "You must be from a large family."

"It's a hotel."

"Oh, fine. That would be the Menger."

"The Angus."

"A new hotel?"

"It's one of the oldest buildings in the city." I often found my-self saying this with the same pride in my voice that my mother had when she spoke of the Angus.

"How terribly clever." With this incongruous expression, she managed to dismiss our whole way of life.

"It's a darling place when you get up there," Wade Howell explained.

At first I was surprised, because of course she had never been to the Angus. Then I was annoyed, because I realized she was defending me.

"I'm sure..." Mrs. Gordon Nickerson gave me a spooky smile and handed me the card in two envelopes. "You're just what the cadets are looking for."

I wasn't at all convinced of this, and it occurred to me that the methods for screening young ladies to entertain our young men in uniform were sloppy. Oh well, at that very moment they were probably being shown colored films on venereal disease. At any rate, Mrs. Gordon Nickerson, having fulfilled one social obligation, turned her attention to Wade Howell.

"Congratulations, my dear, on your engagement."

I was annoyed that she kissed Wade.

"Mother's engagement, you mean."

"Really, my dear, you're terribly hard on your mother."

"I never thought of it that way."

But Mrs. Gordon Nickerson had grown bored with us. "I'll see you both Sunday for tea, now."

"Did you find anything at all—even a little back room someplace?"

This was the first time I had seen Wade Howell without her haughty manner. Without it, she seemed to shed her beauty as well. She stood there without a semblance of charm in her slick white dress and orange shoes. I was reminded of those weary young women who age too quickly under the strain of abuse and anxiety. A new dress is no match for the ravages of living and our precarious relationship to time.

"The cadet wives come first."

Wade Howell nodded and mumbled something incoherent.

"I thought by now you would have patched up the little rift with your mother."

Wade Howell turned away and walked out.

"Everyone should be an orphan brought up in a convent."

I was certain this was for the benefit of Mrs. Gordon Nickerson. Nothing more. Wade Howell seemed to be fighting her way out of a suffocating encasement. Then, halfway down the red-carpeted stairs, she managed a small cry for help.

"I'm the criminal. She irritates me until I hate her. Then I'm the criminal."

I could think of nothing to say, and our fragile cord of communication was severed in an instant.

◆ ◆ ◆

The hot sun rejuvenated Wade Howell somewhat. And what nature couldn't accomplish, Frost's Easter display could. Navy-blue dolls, gathering red, white, and blue eggs, romped about on ruby-eyed rabbits. The store was as sensuous as a page out of Colette. It was all woman. The devastating woman who wiggled her hips and propped up her bosom and played hard to get.

As we stood there intoxicated by the fumes of a thousand and one blends of perfume, two cadets came up from behind and broke the spell. We were sincerely annoyed. This was no place for flesh-and-blood men. They could never measure up to the dreams conjured by this sleek palace of witchery. We hurried back toward Joske's, where housewares, toys, and hardware kept us safely weighted down to earth.

Nothing more was said about our conversation with Mrs. Gordon Nickerson. Even when we stepped from the hot street into the cool, dark Menger Bar for a mug of beer, Wade Howell went on at great length to avoid talking about the interview. Instead I heard the life story of the chair of the Cadet Hostesses. How husband by husband she rose from waitress to society matron. Although Wade was making a great effort to be amusing, my attention constantly shifted to the young army wives in the bar who were strumming up a little daylight romance. They all seemed to have the same habit of reaching inside their blouses from time to time for reassurance that their wedding rings had not fallen from their flimsy gold chains to God know where. I despised their wretched little lives.

By the time we got back to the store, we were sleepy from the beer and the sun, and neither of us thought to make plans for our next meeting. I didn't talk to Wade Howell again for almost two weeks. At the Sunday tea dance, I caught a glimpse of a white dress and a black choker and I waved across the dance floor.

In the meantime, I amused myself by dating Richard Randolph Atlas III, whom I adored in a snobbish sort of fashion, and Tad Withers, whom I detested in the same sort of fashion. Then, too, I managed to dash off a sonnet, "To a Girl in White," for my poetry course.

I slid in and out of the Angus as though I were in debt to the landlady. But why should I attempt to avoid Lillie du Lac? Hadn't I lunched with Wade Howell as she suggested? But I sensed that she expected me to dig about in the subtle nuances and emotional twists of the Colonel's family life. That would take time and skill.

Besides, I didn't wish to make a sharp move that might snap to bits my slender friendship with Wade Howell. My friends up until then had been rather nice bores. Wade Howell was different. With her nothing was drab, nothing was dreary, and nothing was just nice. Except Panama perhaps. Superficially we were different. She was a great beauty while I was merely a pretty girl. She was wealthy beyond belief, and I was almost poor. She apparently had a great deal of worldly knowledge, while I was naive to the point of ridicule. What then did we have in common? We had the same cynical attitude, which set the tone for our entire relationship. We were not burdened with the pretense of enthusiasm. We were not taken in by the small pretension of the phonies. And above all, we were not at all certain that life as it was mapped out for us was worth living. But as long as we were trapped in the vacuum, we were determined to do a thorough job of it.

Still, I hesitated to make a move in her direction. After all, she had done me a favor by introducing me to Mrs. Gordon Nickerson, and it bothered me to be indebted to anyone. Especially someone who might demand so much in return.

◆ THREE ◆

Although the Easter season came early that year, it did not bring with it the abrupt emotional uplift that I had always associated with that time. This was due in part to the soft warm climate. Here we did not need a promise of spring, of better things ahead—we never lost them—in a cold gray winter. Except for a half-hearted blizzard, which might last anywhere from an hour to two days and emptied the stores and streets and discontinued transportation, we lived in a fragrant tropical garden.

Then, too, we were in the midst of a war. We were living as nearly as possible at a constant peak of excitement. There was a song in our hearts in those days. True, it was a melancholy song. But an affected melancholy tempered by confidence. And we enjoyed everything about it.

As I left the store the Saturday before Easter, I was very much aware of the time, the place, and the moment. In the half block from Joske's of Texas to the Alamo, three cadets, a pair of sergeants, and one stunning second lieutenant made futile stabs at last-minute Saturday night dates. But the night was young, I

57

felt hot and messy, and Wade Howell had a crazy notion about hunting for confetti eggs in the Mexican Quarter.

That morning, when she handed me the advertising copy for the Sportshop, I found a little note clipped to the top sheet. It was marked *personal.* Of course, it was from Wade Howell. Even Joske's art department would go to pieces if its artists handled their pencils with such a tight elementary grip. And certainly it was for me. She didn't speak to anyone else in sportswear. Reading the note, I couldn't avoid feeling a little quiver of annoyance. Why should I be destined to jump and run any time this strange girl saw fit to turn her smooth young head in my direction? I was tempted to refuse the invitation when it occurred to me that all I had to look forward to that night was a date with Tad Withers. Then, too, the notion that I was indebted to Wade Howell sucked at me like a leech. I pictured, not entirely unhappily, a blackmail that would go on forever.

I found Wade Howell posed before a display of antique silver. Dark hair, dark glasses, white dress—the cool lady of mystery on the hot streets of a southern city. She looked satisfied.

"Let's freshen up," she said.

I didn't mention the fact that we were only three blocks from the Angus. Instead we pushed past five blocks of soldiers to the Saint Anthony Hotel. In the ladies' lounge, she pulled off her dress, kicked off her shoes, and ran a basin of water all at once.

On the mirrored door there were flimsy depictions of languorous mermaids floating among seaweed that looked curiously like cacti. In a futile attempt to be modern, the artist had disjointed the mermaids so that the effect was more pitiful than decorative. But for an instant, when Wade Howell stood before the mirror, the painting took on the sensuous quality that was intended. One of the fish tails fitted perfectly on her torso. Startled, I let out a little gasping sound before I had time to catch myself. She must have noticed, for she turned her head slightly to give her shoulders and breasts a more seductive quality.

"Come home with me tonight, and we'll swim in the pool." She said this in the hesitant throaty whisper she had adopted as her natural voice. I was accustomed to this affectation by now and usually found it restful in the midst of all the jittery chatter about me. But at that point it disturbed me as much as the invitation.

"I'm sorry," I said, "some other time." And I meant it. I simply wasn't ready.

Wade Howell tossed her shoulder and went back to the business at hand. The next five minutes were a work of art. A few deft movements and the short dark hair was shampooed and dried, the amber body was sponged and dressed, and we were off on a nonsensical escapade.

It was a relief to get away from the plush pink lounge with the lavender mermaids. It was the first time I experienced the curious wave of discontent that I was to come to know so well. The feeling always soared higher and dipped lower when I was in close quarters with this girl. At first I thought it was my own restlessness and boredom with playing second. Not until much later did I realize that I was experiencing the humiliating sensation of feeling unwanted. Wade Howell wanted desperately to be alone with her own precious body.

"Come on, we won't find any eggs in here, and I promised Mother."

"I thought you were having an argument with your family."

"Oh, that—that goes way back. We still have to live through each day together."

"We all have our family arguments," I said inanely.

"Of course, but I'm afraid Mrs. Nickerson gave you the wrong impression."

"Not really. I gathered that it was nothing serious."

"It couldn't be more serious. But at least when we're arguing there's something to hang on to. It's when we stop that I go deeper and deeper into bitter hatred until I think I'll never come up for air."

I let her continue.

"After all, just because she did it and had a baby and I turned out to be the baby is no reason for me to like her. Besides, how do I know she's my mother? Maybe she bought me like she does everything else."

I couldn't manage to strum up an adequate answer on such short notice, but I was aware of a quick splash of anger when I thought of a snot-nosed little waif being torn from its mother on the dusty road of some little tropical outpost. From what I had heard from Lillie, it would not have occurred to Colonel Howell's wealthy wife that anyone could prefer living in poverty to being a sleek shiny heiress. But I must remember that Wade Howell was full of fanciful ideas.

We picked our way over scorching pieces of broken sidewalk until we came to a nasty-looking little café called Kinky and Nando's.

"I'll collapse if I don't have something to eat." Wade Howell had the appetite of a growing boy.

Once inside, I was convinced we had made a mistake. There was nothing to indicate that we were in a restaurant. The sign nailed loosely to the front porch of the house might just as easily have been indicative of a draught outside as it was of food inside. There was a table, although I could barely make it out, in the concentrated spray of light that seeped in from the tiny prison window high on one wall. At least there wasn't the usual fuss over choosing an inconspicuous spot. If we were to be stared at, it would not be openly, and the tablecloth was clean and starched.

Kinky, or was it Nando, came to take our order, or perhaps share a meager meal with two strangers from the hot streets. Whatever it was, he didn't seem surprised that we were there.

"What will the señoritas have?"

When we hesitated, he suggested we leave the choice to him. Then he turned to Wade.

"This is on the house."

"No, I'll pay," I started to protest, but Wade interrupted.

"Money is useless here—at least, my money."

Dishes arrived. I was skeptical, of course. Then I tasted them. Superb! There was a platter of flaming red enchiladas surrounded by a pepper and eggplant mixture, a cool crushed avocado salad, and a pitcher of Mexican beer. The natural food of a hot dry climate.

"It's wonderful, isn't it? Even though sometimes I think the price is a little steep."

"But you said..."

She laughed. Then suddenly she got up.

"I'll only be a minute."

She went over to a young Mexican who had quite suddenly appeared in the light under the window. He was only slightly taller than Wade and just as beautiful. In fact, he was so attractive that I didn't even speculate as to whether he was Kinky or Nando. It was odd, I thought, that he gave no indication of noticing Wade's presence until she touched him lightly on the arm. Then, hand in hand, they disappeared into the back of the café.

It was a good fifteen minutes before Wade came back.

"I'm famished," she announced. The quantity of food that Wade Howell was able to eat was a constant source of amazement to me. That among other things.

"Did you ever get laid by a blind man?" she asked between man-size bites.

I was too dumbstruck to answer immediately. Apparently she thought I was untangling skeletons from a heap of discarded lovers.

"Oh, you'd remember if you had. They're so sensitive—as soon as you touch them, they go wild." Then, after another bite of enchilada and a swallow of beer: "This is the first one I've had."

My thoughts flew off in all directions. The web of illusion had been broken, and there wasn't one fine thread of reason that I could grasp. Once before I had experienced that same overpowering feeling of desolate humiliation that left me so uniquely alone.

I was a backward ten-year-old at the time. And one of my worldly friends took it upon herself to demonstrate what "it was all about," as she put it. It turned out that I was the diagram, and with the aid of a Dr Pepper bottle, it was a very thorough as well as painful demonstration indeed.

Wade Howell wiped her mouth and said, "I think it's the nicest thing the way Kinky is so good to his brother."

"Naturally," I thought, "the bald one would be called Kinky." This minor elation at having untangled an insignificant detail gave me momentary relief from the stifling cloud of gloom that billowed about me.

"He works so hard just so his brother can have a little pleasure."

I wished she would go behind the curtain again, so that I could escape into the street.

"You seem to know them well," was what I said.

"Not really. But I have been here before. Kinky makes the best enchiladas I've ever tasted."

"You apparently have quite a passion for...enchiladas."

Wade Howell laughed. "The medium of exchange is interesting, don't you think? It's so tiresome always dealing in money."

"Tiresome maybe, but a little easier to explain when your parents accuse you of frittering away your allowance."

A quick angry expression that even the darkness could not hide turned Wade Howell's face into a mocking mask of horror.

"Do you think for one minute that she scares me?"

She stood up and continued angrily, "I want her to know what I do. If she's not hurt too, it's all pointless."

At last, it seemed to me that a personal question was in order.

"What are your parents like?" I asked.

"Ordinary...very ordinary."

"The Colonel—is he ordinary?"

"Worse. No, I shouldn't say that. She's made him what he is... nothing. Because of me, he's nothing....She lives through me— we're attached and I'm going to damn well show her we're alive."

On the way to the door, I tripped over a broken piece of linoleum and hurt my knee. Out in the daylight, I saw that the skin was broken and blood was running down my leg.

"Damn it all. If I wash it off, my leg makeup will smear."

I was thankful for the shallow thoughts that always held up as remarkably sound when pitted against the more profound reveries.

We crossed over to the marketplace. The dim room, the dark men, and the trickle of blood were soon forgotten in the flimsy gaiety of primitive pottery, Aztec calendars, and turquoise trinkets.

"I see you have eggs," Wade Howell was saying to an enormous woman with a tiny head that was a mass of pin curls to be unwound on Easter morning.

"A small resurrection," I said aloud.

"What?" Wade Howell had no sense of humor.

"Nothing."

Wade turned back to the monstrous woman in the crepe paper stall.

"How much?"

"Three for ten cents."

"I'll give you ten dollars for all of them."

It was a deal. The fat Mexican woman went happily out of business. As for us, we were piled high with Easter eggs. We each carried two shopping bags full of them, and some were tucked in our pockets and pocketbooks. I even had two pale pink ones, Wade's idea of course, tucked in my bra. She was more fortunate.

Even so, we were reluctant to leave the mellow confusion of the Mexican Quarter. Ever present in the dusty decay was the comforting yet melancholy sense of timelessness. But the sun was setting. And the sad gaiety was more pronounced after dark when the Mexicans mentally threw up their hands and gave up the exhausting struggle of trying to imitate their conquerors. I often wondered, as I got lost against the bleached stucco buildings that silhouetted the Mexicans so well, just who had conquered whom. Now, just at dark, the aroma of a million smoky tortillas blended with the natural fragrance of the air.

Even the poorest Mexican has the natural dignity to dine late, I thought.

They would know, of course, that at eight o'clock every night the wind blew in from across the plains and swept away the last traces of the odorous evening meal. Then they were free to revel in taste without the confusion of smell.

"We can always come back," Wade Howell said. "It's not as though we were very far away. Anyway, you have a date."

"Yes."

"Anything interesting?"

"Not exactly contagious."

"Why do you waste your time?"

Why indeed? I couldn't tolerate Tad Withers. Where Robert Parker vaguely annoyed me, Tad Withers disgusted me to the point of nausea. And there was Richard Randolph Atlas III, whom I almost liked. But still I chose to go out with the detestable Tad Withers. There was one consolation: it was relaxing.

That's it, I thought happily. I don't give a damn what he thinks of me.

With this sudden clear feeling of mild happiness, I followed Wade Howell onto a bus called Culebra, which took us on a wild ride over the twisting streets. At one particularly reckless corner, Wade fell into the lap of the bus driver.

"Now, honey," he said, "if you all'd listen to what I told you and moved to the back of the bus . . ."

But neither the driver nor Wade seemed in a hurry to untangle the shapely legs from the money box. The fragile paper eggs that we had gone to so much trouble to find were forgotten. And pink and green and yellow transfers mingled with the confetti to emphasize the curiously festive feeling ordinary public service buses took on in this city.

Once we were downtown again, Wade Howell turned her face to the window and said, "I guess you think I'm awful, but I have the feeling she's with me all the time."

I got up to change buses.

"Do you think I could come and stay with you?"

Fortunately there wasn't time to say what I thought. In fact, when I got off, I realized there wasn't even time to go home and change. Across the street the jewelers' clock said 8:30. Saturday night and there I stood in the middle of Houston Street with two shopping bags of Wade's Easter eggs, a bloody leg, and a strangely lopsided bosom.

"I'll meet you at 2:30 ... tomorrow ... at the Orangeana," Wade Howell called from the window.

A soldier stepped up and asked me who my girlfriend was. I backed into the shadow of the two dark brooding Mexicans who were leaning on the building.

◆ FOUR ◆

I decided to store the eggs in a locker at the Greyhound bus terminal. I could put on a new face in the restroom and not have to go home before my date. There might even be time to sit down and rest for a few minutes. Since I had taken to wearing spectator pumps instead of the saddle shoes that were permitted in the Sportshop, I felt tired at night. Then, too, chasing the streets with Wade Howell was a good deal more demanding than lounging around reading Keats, Byron, Shelley, and Dos Passos.

Thinking of the pile of unopened books and blank papers lying in a neglected heap, I felt a stab of regret. But then I could always get back to that after I had "lived a little." Exactly what constituted this "living" business, I wasn't quite sure. I supposed that for the time being, at least, it meant having a few affairs... a sort of indoctrination period into the pseudo-sophisticated world of sex. The ever-present, much-heralded world that had somehow found me wanting... until lately at least. Well, I would show it. After all, I wasn't so bad. I had a slim figure and pretty legs, which the new high heels showed off to advantage. And the blond streak that shot across my brown hair dramatized my dark eyebrows and wide forehead. Men were noticing me lately, too—even when I wasn't with Wade Howell.

It never occurred to me that the reason for this recent attention was natural rather than synthetic. I had quite suddenly lifted my head and accepted what I saw. Perhaps it was just as well that I didn't recognize the danger in this tardy metamorphosis, for then it might have been a source of anxiety rather than a source of enjoyment. And during that long summer season, I might have stayed hidden behind the shutters instead of soaking up the sunlight.

The bus station was a mess. And there were no empty lockers. I would have to wait until someone checked out. I found a seat in the midst of the happy confusion of a Mexican family traveling with their unusual assortment of paper bags, live chickens, and beautiful children.

Then, as I was taking off my shoes, I spied aviation cadet Richard Randolph Atlas III. He was heading for the lockers. As luck would have it, he had the key for number nineteen. I desperately wanted that locker, but I certainly didn't want him to see me in my present frowzy condition. I would never be quite ready for Richard Randolph Atlas III.

As soon as he had taken the bulging briefcase from number nineteen and safely turned his back, I edged in behind him with one of the paper bags hiding my face. And for a moment, I felt foolishly accomplished in my trivial mission. But I couldn't resist a sly peek at the mysterious briefcase. What in the name of

heaven made such rocky bumps? In that slip of a second, a casual crowd of overprivileged oil heiresses slid their tennis rackets
into my locker. Their shrill voices hardly matched their slippery
movements. But I held the key.

Of course, Richard Randolph Atlas III heard the commotion.
He turned toward me.

"Well, now, I sure am glad to run across you again, Jane Davis."

His voice bubbled over with polite concern. But everything
was all wrong. Surely this fluorescent scene would mellow into
something more appropriate, and I would find myself in proper
crinoline flowing down a wide winding staircase to greet my gen-
tleman friend.

Instead, I stood there flustered and shabby while the sport
queens took over locker nineteen and then started in on Richard
Randolph Atlas III with "isn't this a small world" chatter.

It's uncanny, I thought, how they can smell each other out
from one end of the country to the other.

"Haven't I seen you someplace?"

"That's entirely possible. I've always been one place or
another."

"Don't you just love his sense of humor?"

"Did you say you went to Virginia?"

"That's it—one Easter week."

"Now don't tell me . . . it was '39, or maybe '40."

"They wear jackets and ties at that place, and honey, I didn't
even wear shoes until the army got me to."

"He's a riot, an absolute riot."

"Y'all have me mixed up with the Virginia Randolphs on my mother's side...let me see...eight, maybe ten times...in fact you could say entirely removed, since Ma had to marry the old man. Yeh, she got mixed up with Clem Atlas from Atlas Hollow when she was not much more than twelve years old. Didn't know no better. Seeing what happened to Ma made me determined to get me a smart educated girl like Jane here."

He led me gently away, and we sat in a clutter of spittoons, candy wrappers, and comic books watching the nubby thick-soled one-generation heiresses file out, subdued but not defeated.

◆ FIVE ◆

Richard Randolph Atlas III was undoubtedly the handsomest, richest, most eligible boy I had ever dated. He was from Raleigh, North Carolina, and his family were "up to their asses," according to Mrs. Gordon Nickerson, in tobacco and money. And young Richard, brought up in the noble southern tradition of wide porticoes and tall drinks, would have gallantly sacrificed all that for a wretched little charmer he had picked up on the streets of San Antonio. He was madly in love with me, or so he said.

As he put it: "Jane Davis, I just love girls who do something, and you're the only one who evah turned her little finger to do anything."

This, of course, was flattering—in a limited way, but, to be perfectly honest, I didn't quite believe that he meant anything permanent to come of this somewhat gloomy infatuation, so I dismissed the whole thing with the face-saving excuse that I wasn't quite ready to settle down with a rich handsome husband.

I was being more honest than I knew. An unseasonable transplant to a lush landscape sheltered from the sun would be a deadly move for the cactus that flowers in the desert, where the only excesses are repellent and severe. I could love the image of Dick alone, but I couldn't fancy us as a couple, for even a vision of the pampered matron was offensive to me. The time hadn't come for me to settle down with a rich and handsome husband.

I didn't even feel quite comfortable about having a modestly good time. This guilt was a holdover from the bleak cold days of the Depression when the long gray lines quickly scratched through the hardly realized moments of color…the long winter dream played out against an always nightmarish backdrop of black and white. Ironic indeed that it took another nightmare, the red and gold blast of war, to make us rub our eyes and become accustomed once again to a brilliant spectacle. The unfamiliar color dulled our senses to the horror. We were enjoying ourselves for the first time in a decade. This was the carnival time of life, and we intended to celebrate, and celebrate we did, although a bit uneasily and self-consciously.

"I was on my way to something long and cool," he said. "Care to join me?"

"Sorry, I have a date waiting someplace in town." I looked at the shopping bags. "I didn't want to come dressed as a paper bag."

"You just leave the detail to me and rest your poor little ol' feet."

I sat back with my toes in my heels and watched Richard Randolph Atlas III all but charm the pants off a Texas tavern tramp while they dug around together among the litter in her handbag. Before they found the key, I found myself wishing that the dirty woman would get on her bus and go. And by the time Richard Randolph Atlas III had the eggs safely tucked away in the locker, I had been still long enough to collect my exhaustion, and I thought briefly of forgetting about the detestable Tad Withers and drifting aimlessly through the night with this cool, smooth cadet. Seconds later, I woke up to the sensation of a clean hard shoulder.

"Honey, you sure as heck need someone to look after you."

"What time is it? How long have we been like this?"

"Have you always been all charged up like this, or is it having all those Yankees around ruined you?"

The fact that I had established residence below the Mason-Dixon Line made me acceptable to Cadet Richard Randolph Atlas III—geographically at least.

"You're provincial—that's what you are. And just when I was beginning to like you."

"You'd like me fine if you evah got a night's rest."

It struck me that maybe he was right. In order to fully savor Richard Randolph Atlas III, I needed a clear head and more time than I cared to devote to one man. His voice was so low and his speech so slow that our on-the-run relationship did not work to his advantage. Besides, he was not part of the mood of the times. His values were steady and permanent, and he refused to be taken in by the jaunty, swaggering heroics of a nation that seemed to shrug off a world catastrophe with "We'll win this little fight in style." As for me, I was determined to be of the moment. At least, this was the intricate line of reasoning that I used to protect myself from this prince. But now, in the stinking bus station, my argument was falling to pieces.

"Honey, our youth is a wastin' away—let's get out of this filthy hole."

"You've convinced me, but only one drink."

"Then...?"

"I told you. I have a date."

"Couldn't you concentrate your patriotism? It's not doing any of us any good sprinkled over the whole damn army."

By the time we reached La Tapatia, we were in a hilarious mood. We went out back and sat on a tiny terrace. Through a broken wall, we looked out onto Travis Street. Richard Randolph Atlas III opened his briefcase and took out a bottle of Old Grand-Dad as though it were the Medal of Honor. We ordered soda to show we were sports, but he insisted on water with the precious bourbon. I leaned back and thought, They will never be able to take all the romance out of this place...no matter what they do.

"I don't think you know what a beautiful girl you are."

"Oh?"

"You look the way movies think the average girl looks—but they don't look that way."

Dick moved from his side of the table, and we sat close holding hands and talking about our first meeting. There was only the recent past in those days. Anything before was childhood. The war came and a whole generation grew up. Or tried to.

"I thought those tea dances were for the birds until I met you."

I loved the tea dances, although I had only been to one. The long innocuous Sunday afternoon seemed a perfect ending to a dizzy weekend. With new cadets every nine weeks, the dances seemed the very essence of the transiency that pervaded the times—fantastically unreal, admittedly transparent relations. But no one let down their hair. The girls were coolly desirable and warmly hospitable, and the men were stiff-mannered tin soldiers. The picture appealed to me.

I remembered I had felt headily popular when, arriving late, Mrs. Nickerson greeted me with: "I've been waiting for you. I have this lovely boy who'll be just right for you."

After Cadet Richard Randolph Atlas III briefed me on his background, I wondered what wacky system for "pairing off" the fabulous Mrs. Nickerson was experimenting with. Perhaps she referred to her own rocky background when in doubt. Anyway, Cadet Richard Randolph Atlas III seemed satisfied, and quite possibly that was her object.

As I sat close to Dick on the splintery bench at La Tapatia, I could almost feel the hot beery breaths passing in the street. Dick was pushing the hair behind my ear and gently blowing pretty thoughts into it, and nothing else mattered.

"Pretty ears…you have the prettiest ears and the most beautiful legs."

I was content. But perhaps it was only my tiredness that allowed me to be satisfied with this gentleness.

"You're very sweet, but I have to leave you now."

We got up without a word and danced our way across the terrace out onto the sidewalk. I stumbled over a soldier propped against the dirty yellow wall. His face was smeared with blood, and blood ran down the corners of his mouth. He lifted his head and tried to speak, but he collapsed from the pain. Two MPs came and dragged him into a jeep. I felt sick.

Dick led me down the stone stairs to the river, where we sat silently watching a family of Mexicans picnicking in a party boat.

"You're a prettier color now. I can turn you loose."

I smiled and felt very tender.

"What a funny little girl you are. You know, when I watch you walk away, I always get the feeling that you're going to turn a corner and never be heard of again."

Dick held my face between his hands and kissed me sweetly. As he pressed against me, I felt the paper egg break in my pocket, and all the rest of the night, confetti seeped out through a tiny hole in my dress and left a crazy trail around the city.

◆　◆　◆

I did not remember that Sergeant Tad Withers had gray hair. His face was young, but he was certainly gray. We met under the bright lights of the Gunter Hotel, so I couldn't have been mistaken. At first this fascinated me, after a while it seemed quite ordinary, and finally I was annoyed.

"We are meeting another couple," Tad was saying.

I longed for Dick, and his refined breath in my ear. I detested other couples. I wondered what passing fancy had prompted me to make this date. Possibly a momentary fascination with maturity. It would necessarily be fleeting, for as a rule, my whole nature rebelled against growing up. As long as I could remember, I was distinctly aware of the passage of time.

"I'll introduce you as an old friend from Detroit—I sold to stores there," the gray bird was saying.

It was worse than I expected. The other couple were married. Claire and Burt Newcomb, for God's sake. And I was playing this insane farce for the benefit of their dreary conventionality.

I was introduced to a big girl with big feet and big hands who must have been told she had a wonderful personality, for she went in for personality in a big way. Her husband was tall and thin and looked intellectual but was not.

"I feel like a character out of Dos Passos," I said, hoping to make this pale hawk flap his wings and fly. My loneliness was so desperate in the midst of the glare and noise of the hotel lobby that any fragile link of momentary understanding seemed desirable. But the wave of panic passed, and no one noticed, much less responded. The rough hand of the gray sergeant steered me by the elbow across the street and down a treacherous flight of stairs to a gloomy hangout known as the International Club. The name and four murals, two Scandinavian and two Spanish, were the inspiration of a Mexican sign painter who was also the owner. His three-hundred-pound wife acted as cashier and bouncer. It was rumored that they were also responsible for the Blue Room and the Mona Lisa, the only after-hours spots in the city. If so, I forgave them for this dreary cavern—if for no other reason than to hear the Mexican girls sing "Mona Lisa." They gave it a quick little gasping lilt that sizzled crazily through the streets. After a certain hour, this whispering sound seemed to reverberate around every corner. Mona Lisa...Mona Lisa...Mona Lisa.

A fat finger pointed to a table next to two aviation cadets and a fifth of Canadian Club. I kicked my way through the sawdust in a hurry to get the seat facing them. At least there was something to amuse me besides that gray head and a Swedish milkmaid.

Since no one was carrying a bottle, we ordered beer at our table, and I looked longingly at the Canadian Club.

"It was certainly a coincidence you two meeting in this Godforsaken place—and speaking of the long arm of you know what, how are Sheila and the children?"

Sheila was no concern of mine. I was ashamed of being with these people for reasons of my own. Godforsaken indeed! Their suffocating boxed-in lives slipped past in a series of flash slides: dusty mahogany tables, garish lamps, sticky children, boiled potatoes, and bridge tables. I could have cheerfully slashed that comfortable woman's tongue. Places were always more important to me than people.

"Fine, fine. You see I met Miss Davis when I was selling around the Detroit area. It's a small world, I always say."

"Oh, you're the one."

"She works here now. Right over there at that big store by the Alamo. I was just passing through—brushing up, so to speak. You never know—this war might be over some day, and we'll have to get back to work."

"You don't have to make any apologies."

"Who's apologizing? I just thought it was interesting."

"Oh, the small-world routine."

"Now listen, don't go getting any ideas. You can see right here in her shoe."

I was glad my shoes were lying under the table; otherwise I am certain he would have snatched them off my feet. Instead he sifted the sawdust out, letting it drift here and there, some in our beer, some floating off onto other tables. No one seemed to care enough to start a fuss. The cadets were staring in our direction, but they were too beady-eyed from the bottle to respond to petty annoyances. Anyway, they were being entertained by the performance at our table. No doubt they were discussing our relationship.

While Claire picked bits of dust from her beer with a fingernail file, her husband sat immobile. He had not stirred since we came in the place. He was so withdrawn that he did not even stare. I decided that I had never seen anyone who could remain so motionless, and I wondered what he did for the army. Not so Gray Top, who was charged with insignificant movement. I thought he was going to scratch right through the soles of my shoes.

"Those shoes have been around since the last time you looked in them," I said. "It wouldn't surprise me if what you're looking for isn't on the bottom of my foot."

I remembered the first time he looked into my shoe. It was at the non-com club, and it seemed like a sweet tenderness then, and I felt a little thrill. I thought I sensed a gentle loneliness about him that might appeal to me. Now, in this hideous dive and in the company of his dreary friends, he was a dirty little man, and I felt ashamed.

"Les all have a little drink together." The dark cadet with the wiry hair was standing over us, extending the Canadian Club by way of introduction. He was tall, and although his eyes were bloodshot and his smile distorted, he had clean good looks that I admired. Nothing about him was spectacular, but he did shine. For the first time since I had slipped from the bus into the numbing atmosphere of restless tranquility, I felt the weight of my lifelessness lift.

"We can push our tables together an have a little party."

"We're having a party, soldier."

"I beg your pardon. This is my first time off the post, and I'm carried away with good will."

My gray date certainly did not wish to have his manners shown up, since they were an essential part of the elaborate fabrication he carried on.

"Meet the Newcombs and my wife." I looked at the cadet with a crooked twist of a smile and said nothing.

"I'm Gerald Eaton and this is Donald Swarthout. May I have the next dance with your wife?"

He was right out of my world and he was a slick one. The gray daddy had no choice. After all, this was a lonesome confused soldier in a strange city. Let the boy have a little fun. As for me, I popped up so fast that even Sergeant Newcomb had to rouse himself to save his beer bottle from the floor. Lonesome home-sick indeed. I was fascinated.

We danced to "Sleepy Time Down South."

"This is my favorite," he said.

I said nothing.

"I've never had a preference until a few minutes ago."

"I'm glad you asked me to dance."

"I watched you come in."

"I know."

"I watched every move you made."

"Yes."

"I have to be back on the post in exactly forty-five minutes. It takes a half hour to get there."

"We have fifteen minutes."

"Maybe. If you're married to that old guy, I promised Swarthout we'd finish the bottle."

"You can go back to your bunk half sober."

We stood apart and looked at each other for a moment. A PFC and a corporal were arguing about whose nickel was to play "San Fernando Valley." We danced through it twice in silence. Then, when it was almost over, he kissed the top of my head, and I looked up.

"What's your name?"

"Jane Davis."

"Jane, I'm a very lucky guy. Tomorrow, if my luck holds out, I will be back in town. Where can I see you?"

"The Gunter Hotel."

"Good enough."

He took out a pen and something that looked like a snapshot. While he wrote, I looked at him and wondered how I could live until tomorrow. Then he tucked the message into my pocket and came out with a handful of confetti.

"Happy new year!"

It was a sweet kiss that brought on such a nasty row. The sergeant was ready to defend his pride, with sleeves rolled up to his stripes. Swarthout was ready to sacrifice the precious Canadian Club if called upon to act as second. Gerald Eaton was ready to leave.

"You have a lovely wife. Take care of her."

He said he was sorry the sergeant misunderstood, but it was all in fun, and he walked out as though he had thanked one and all for a splendid party in his honor.

"I don't like guys who horn in."

I felt the rough hand on my elbow. After so much, I couldn't go back to this. I grabbed what was left of the confetti and threw it in his face. Then I ran up the stairs of the International Club and got lost in the crowds. I was almost home when I remembered the two shopping bags of confetti eggs.

◆　◆　◆

The bus station was at least as crowded as it was earlier. But there was a difference. Then there had been overtones of gaiety brought about by frantically brief Saturday night plans. Now there were undertones of desperation precipitated by the faces of an entirely different crowd. Young army wives and their unhealthy babies and old Mexican women in black shawls on unhealthy religious pilgrimages. I wondered why the men never found solace in those missions of discomfort. Praise be to the Greyhound bus company and the Texas Highway Department for lightening the burden of these weary sinners.

In the short time it had taken me to get the shopping bags, the streets had become deserted. The street cleaners were doing their work. It was as though the monstrous sweeper had sucked up a city of dolls. I had the night to myself.

I swerved suddenly and crossed Houston Street by the Texas Theatre and went down the stairs to the river. It was cooler down there in the midst of the lush shrubbery. Although the usual light wind had blown in at eight thirty, the hot Saturday night crowds had kept the sidewalks from cooling off. My plan was to follow the river, stopping every now and then to rest on a stone bench until I reached the stairway at Commerce and Losoya. There, with luck and perseverance, I would cross a crazy five-point intersection, which was no worse than dozens of legalized death traps where madmen went around on wheels, but tired as I was, I dreaded it.

As I wandered aimlessly in the recent past dreaming about the kisses of Gerald Eaton, I felt someone come up behind me. The steps were in sight, but I couldn't make a run for them without spilling eggs all over the place, so I kept up a stiff uncomfortable pace. I felt that my pursuer was gaining on me, but perhaps this was only my imagination taking advantage of my exhaustion.

All at once there was a moment of complete calm. The breeze surrounded me with one last playful caress and blew off. The tortured tires on the melted street above stopped shrieking in the night. Then, just as I put my foot on the first step, I thought I heard familiar sounds in the distance. It was Jess playing the guitar and singing "Don't Fence Me In." I heard a boisterous laugh and clapping to the melody. That would be Mira, and I pictured her sullen husband grooming himself in the background.

A pair of strong arms met in a firm grip around my breasts. "Underneath the starry above," Jess was singing. Then the insane drivers took over in a mad chase of death. I felt a bony chin on my head and a hard chest against my back. I was so stupefied with fright and exhaustion that I didn't think to drop the shopping bags and free my hands for the struggle. Wild fancies spun in and out of my head and I did nothing to resist the attack. The street noises became shrill and jerky, as though I were poking a finger in and out of my ear, while down below all was still and peaceful. Strange.

Then I saw my attacker. He was a soldier, young but frightening. He shoved me up against a fountain and stared at me. No one had ever looked at me like that before. Stripped of any pretense at communication, we were hardly more than snarling animals. I turned my head toward the fountain, but the sunny western limestone was a monster. My dress was pulled up, and he was rubbing against me. I screamed, and he stuck his tongue in my mouth, and I bit it so hard that I must have chewed off a piece. But I couldn't tell, for I spit so much blood into the monster's watery face that it hid everything else. The young soldier started to curse and run around in circles. I should have run away right then, but instead I started slamming him around with the shopping bags. I was so hot that I looked down at my feet to see if they were on fire. At that moment my attacker gave me a slight push (by this time he was pretty tired) intended to topple me into the San Antonio River. Fortunately a norther blew up with such force that it pushed me back from the edge of the river, and as I teetered precariously on the edge of the walk that had been lovingly donated by the Texas Historical Society, I watched my Social Security card and the Eaton family disappear down the river in a floating garden of confetti. I ran up the stairs and stood shivering on the corner waiting for the lights to change. "Give me land, lots of land." There was not a sign of the storm that raged below, but I couldn't help but feel that my attacker would have succeeded had he struck in the confusion of the streets. The soothing notion that my destiny was not altogether in my own hands gave me a comfortable feeling, and I felt a strange aching pity for the young soldier.

And once more I came back to the little courtyard behind the Angus Hotel.

"I had a nosebleed," I announced.

They all looked at me for a moment with vague beery grins and went back to what they were doing. It was hardly a party, just some lonesome people who had been thrown together by the war. They had all adopted the somewhat distracted, somewhat melancholy attitude of having been snatched from something more important by time and geography. This in turn separated me from the others, because I felt very much a part of the present. There would be no intimate talk with Lillie du Lac that night.

My mother and Lillie du Lac were sitting in a corner talking to Wally McCane, a thin, dark-haired mess sergeant. He seemed frail and pale, leaning as he was against the stone wall between the two work-hardened women—even though for over a week now Lillie du Lac had been on a *Vogue* diet of grapes and gin and 7 Up and had lost ten pounds, according to her own calculation; it seemed to me the only thing she had lost was her high spirits. I had a curious fleeting impression that they were fussing over him with strong potions to sustain life for a few last moments rather than prodding him with beer to keep him in their midst as long as possible. They were both quite fond of Sergeant Wally McCane. Especially my mother. She had given him the large corner room that had once been the trysting place for a Mexican general and his beautiful mistress—according to my mother, at least.

"I don't care what you say; there's not a celebration in the country can compare with the Cotton Carnival." Sergeant McCane was from Memphis. Lillie du Lac spoke up for Mardi Gras, and my mother praised the Fiesta San Jacinto to the sky.

"How would you know?" my mother said. "As long as I've known you, you haven't looked past the bottom of a glass."

"I get to work every day, don't I?"

"All I can say is that it's a good thing you're in the army. No legitimate business would put up with you."

This was their love talk. Rather mild, of course, but then

Sergeant McCane and my mother did not seem as desperately pressed by time as Romeo and Juliet or Tristan and Isolde, nor as cunningly contriving as Lillie du Lac and the Colonel. Sergeant McCane prided himself on his drinking and his open disregard for the army. My mother was flattering him.

"Listen to how your mama talks to me." He looked at me with one of those hopelessly red-eyed looks.

It was a credit to our soft-hearted army that they found a place for him. In a way, he showed his appreciation, because he always kept his shoes shined and his belt buckle polished.

"What you got in the shopping bags?"

"Eggs...confetti eggs." I handed him one.

"I wish I'd sent Suzy some of these. She'd get a kick out of them."

The times he thought of his little daughter were always too late. The day after Christmas he would find the big doll, the woolly bathrobe, or the bunny-fur mittens that "Suzy would get a kick out of."

"You can have these."

"I'll wait and get her something when they come down." He turned to my mother again. "I keep writing Laura about the nice big room."

"I've heard that before." My mother didn't like talking about Laura. "You've been saying that ever since you took the room. The way women have you fooled! I'll tell you what I think—Laura's just putting you off. She has no intention of leaving her job and coming down to a little two-bit hotel."

This was the first time I had heard my mother break down and admit that the Angus Hotel was anything less than an ancestral palace. Sergeant McCane was far from perceptive, but this was an obvious slip. He could see it in my confusion when I began babbling about the egg hunt. He too preferred the smooth plain of pretense and its safe distance from actuality. He steered the subject back to our safe little playground, where Jess was still singing "Don't Fence Me In" to Mira.

"Look at that, will you? If she don't look like a cotton picker." Sergeant McCane had never liked Mira, who was all woman and no pretense.

Mira Faraday had draped her lanky body around the circular bench under the huisache tree in a serpentine pose, ending with her long pale hair hanging over Jess's guitar while her young husband sat on the wall cleaning his fingernails.

"She sure is a cute little ol' mess," as Jess put it. All the men went for her in a big way, although on a somewhat temporary basis—I liked to think. Her husband was apparently the one exception.

Cadet Thomas Faraday was a doll. He had great moist brown eyes, a small elegant nose, flat ears, and a beautifully passionate mouth. The only trouble was he was very short and had a terrible nervous habit of constantly looking over his shoulder. I had never heard him say a word, but according to Lillie du Lac, he had talked too much one night at a roadside tavern outside of Paris, Illinois, and had ended up marrying Mira, "who could have been had for the price of a hotel room," as Lillie du Lac put it.

"But then men are such fools in the company of women," she added.

Tommy Faraday had lived with his bride only a month when he went off to the army. He didn't bother to write, and Mira lost track of him. Except for the baby, she might have forgotten him altogether, since her life was a series of stubby little half-forgotten episodes anyway. But with such a substantial reminder throwing glaring reality into her sluggish days, she relived the brief month of wild passion over and over. And instead of forgetting her inconsequential little husband, his memory blew up out of all proportion to her incipient impression of him—after all, they had latched onto each other expecting nothing more binding than an interesting though temporary bedfellow. With this vision of her love before her, Mira set out on a rough and resourceful trail across the country in search of what she thought she had lost.

Along the way she left the baby with a lovely old farm couple in Oklahoma, stocking their pantry with Carnation milk and dextrose and promising to send them money as soon as she was settled and working. They were sweet and understanding and convinced that a wife's place was beside her husband. Mira was still wrapped up in this substantial pose when she climbed down from a produce truck on the outskirts of San Antonio where another hitchhiker was leaning on his cane at the fork in the road.

Suddenly Tommy Faraday put his fingernail file away, said goodnight, and went back to the army post. Everyone felt relieved, especially Mira. It was always at this point that she felt the urge to weave back through her pitiful little past. Jess put aside his guitar.

"Do you remember—," and she was off on the universal pastime—"what you said when you saw me there in the road with that silly rooster?"

"Sometimes I think, well...and then again, I just don't know," Jess replied.

"And you had the Hawaiian thing around your neck."

"A lei."

"And you were carrying a stalk of bananas over your shoulder."

"And you were so hungry you couldn't take your eyes off of them."

"After you had stuffed me with bananas, you asked me my name."

"Mira, you said."

"Mmm, you said."

"I see such a pretty picture when I hear a name like that... Mira."

Now Jess paused a moment, and I knew he was conjuring up the harsher wind of January when they met, but even pain is sweetened by time, and the present can offer no substitute. He welcomed back that sad New Year's Eve.

"You know, most sounds leave me cold, but every so often something pops out, a name or a phrase, that makes a whole picture...sometimes a whole world. Then for days I think about it. I have to tear myself away, or I'd get lost in it."

Mira stared at him. "You feel all right? I mean, nothing happened to you in the war or anything?"

"I fired a couple of rounds of ammunition at the moon, but I didn't get any answer."

"What about that thing on your face?"

"A personal matter."

"Does it hurt?"

"Not now. Somehow it doesn't seem so personal anymore."

They settled back on their battered luggage, two weary war-time travelers, and went on with the sweet time-killer of bringing each other up to date.

"I guess I had it coming to me. I had no business going down to Mexico on one foot."

Mira turned away tearfully.

"Hey, if that's the way it's gonna be, I'm going right on back to Mexico. That's one place they know how to treat a poor torn-up sailor. They don't turn their heads away and cry. They look right at you straight with those sad eyes that haven't shed tears for a million years because the winds are hot on their faces and the bundles are heavy on their backs.

"Their clay skins are too much a part of the dirt they walk on to get all shook up over a foot buried somewhere in Hawaii."

"You're crazy."

"That's better."

"I've heard those Mexican girls are pretty."

"The one I knew was ugly as sin. But there was a sweet little bar that went with her...that was about the prettiest little setup I've ever run into."

"Was it hard to make her understand you?"

"We got along better before she began to understand me. Everything was real primitive. After I learned Mexican, it was like with any other girl—I was always putting my foot in it."

"What about him—the guy who hurt your face?"

"Her brother. We understood each other right away."

"I know what it means to be in love."

"Love? With that faggot? She just appealed to my practical nature. She sure had a head for business. Why, she even saved all the beer cans and had a little factory out back where she turned out curios for the tourists.... I'll miss her all right. It was always a place to go."

"That's what I want more than anything—a place of my own."

"What burns me up is the ten bucks I spent on these Spanish lessons."

And still no cars came. They untied the rooster's legs, but he didn't go away. Instead he stood there in the deserted road, silhouetted against the moon, and tried to get his bearings. He was a proud and beautiful bird, speckled black and white with long fluffy feathers. But he had been tied up too long, and his new freedom confused him.

"What are you going to do with him?" Jess asked.

"I don't know. I wish he'd go away."

"He won't—he wants someone to take care of him."

"I didn't want to take care of him, but the truck drivers made me. They wanted to give me a present, and that's all they had. They were nice. They kept me going with hamburgers and coffee all along the way."

"Hey, little girl, are you broke?"

"Well, I haven't much money left...traveling is so expensive."

Jess reached into his pocket, pulled out some bills, and handed them to Mira. She drew back as though he were trying to stab her.

"I couldn't."

"If I gave it to you in hamburgers, would you take it?"

"That's different."

"We'll call it a loan. Maybe you can do something for me someday." He dumped the money in her lap.

"Thanks. Thanks a million." Mira started to cry. "Everyone has been so swell."

"Hey, cut it out."

"First the truck drivers and then you."

"For cry sake!"

"Do you have to swear like that?"

"I'm not used to being in the company of ladies." He turned to her with his sweet and devilish grin.

"What's so funny?"

"You—riding across the country in a ten-ton poultry truck and still worrying about being proper."

"I only came from Tulsa by truck; the rest of the way I rode the bus."

"All the difference in the world." Jess settled back and closed his eyes. Then, suddenly: "Say, what are you doing out here in the middle of the road anyway?"

"Looking for my husband."

"Where have you looked besides in trucks and buses?"

"I haven't started looking yet. I know he's someplace around here, though. He's in the air force."

"That narrows it down. Is it anyone special?"

"I'm not chasing after men, if that's what you mean. I'm not that kind of girl."

"Now, what would ever give me that idea?"

Mira was annoyed by his implication and ignored him.

"It's going to be a nice day," Jess said, trying to smooth over the edgy feeling.

"It's early in the morning and the first of January and it's already hot."

"You won't mind the heat once your blood thins out."

"All I can say is, I hope it doesn't take long."

"That depends on your constitution." He looked at Mira. "It won't take you long." He unfastened the strap on his books and settled back to read by flashlight.

"What's that you're reading?"

"*A Farewell to Arms*—I thought it was appropriate."

"We had a list of books to read in high school, but I'd rather read magazines—something true to life . . . like *True Confessions.*"

"I've lived better ones than they have in there, and I've only just started."

All at once the rooster crowed and it was morning and reality set in.

"Still not a car in sight," Jess said.

"I don't care. Now that I'm this far, I'm scared."

"Say, does that guy have any idea you're coming?"

"No. I thought I'd surprise him."

"You will."

"He was supposed to send for me when he got here, but with the mails so undependable . . ."

"If all the letters that are thought to be lost were put in one pile, and those that are received put in another pile, I'd give you eight to five the first pile would be twice as big as the second pile."

"You don't believe he wrote to me."

"Personally I'm a great believer in lost letters."

"You're crazy."

An old blue DeSoto went screaming by into the sunrise, came to a short stop, and then weaved back to pick up the hitchhikers. A wonderful drunk Mexican soldier leaned out into the soft pink dawn and said, "Y'all going to San Antone?"

During a long peppery hospitable meal at a blue-and-white-tiled restaurant that belonged to the soldier's family, Mira and Jess were introduced to three grandmothers, six aunts, and ten sisters. The drunk soldier was apparently the only surviving male in the Cortez family, which went clear back to Hernando Cortez. Well, if he wasn't quite so dashing as his mighty ancestor, he was sweet.

Somewhere between the enchiladas and the frijoles, it was decided that Mira should stay at the Angus Hotel until she found her husband and they could make more permanent arrangements together.

At first this didn't go over at all with my mother and Lillie du Lac. And as my mother said, "You can hardly have blamed us."

"You should have seen them," Lillie du Lac said.

Jess and Mira would have dropped the subject right there, but my mother and Lillie du Lac had entered the picture and would have none of that.

"She was wearing a T-shirt," Lillie went on, "with bare legs and carrying that old suitcase tied with a rope and a chicken under her arm."

I looked at Mira Faraday, and I had to admit that there was that frank earthiness about the girl that made her instantly attractive to men.

"And there was our sailor," Lillie du Lac made one of her sweeping gestures, which seemed to take in not only Jess but the entire navy blocked out in chorus behind him, "who went away so long ago and came back a man."

"At least part of one," Jess said.

We all looked uncomfortably at nothing in particular until the difficult moment was over. Fortunately for the rest of us, Jess rarely mentioned his disability; his nature was to make light of things.

"With that Hawaiian thing around his neck."

"A lei."

"They were a sight when they came into the courtyard that morning—New Year's Day it was, too."

"Throwing banana peels all over the place," my mother said. "They even knocked the blossom off the century plant—after I'd waited seven years to see it bloom."

"You could hardly blame us for the way we acted."

And now they were all four safely back in January playing an old familiar game.

"Is that yours? Are you—?" my mother asked, nodding toward Mira.

"Jess, I expected something more original from you...like

one of those pretty Hawaiian girls." This, of course, was Lillie du Lac.

"It's nothing like that. We only met a couple of hours ago on the outskirts," Jess explained. "This is Mira—"

"Faraday."

"This is my mother and Lillie du Lac, a friend of the family."

"*The* friend of the family," Lillie said.

"I've heard so much about you that I feel as though I know you," Mira said inanely.

"Thank God it was only two hours."

"I didn't get the name," Mira said to Lillie.

"Lillie du Lac, New Orleans French."

"Mira's looking for her husband."

"That doesn't surprise anyone," Lillie said.

"I'm terribly anxious to find him, but first I want to wash my hair."

"Maw, if you could put her up, she's had a hard trip."

"I believe it," said Lillie du Lac, studying Mira.

"I don't know," my mother hesitated. "Lately I've had all I can do with the transients coming in off the street. They're better pay than permanents—and they're not always asking for extra towels and soap."

"I'll only be here until I find my husband."

"Martha doesn't like renting to women. It cheapens a place, she always says." Lillie du Lac turned to my mother. "Do you remember that waitress in number three, the one with the smelly feet? Always hanging little laundries in the window. After her came the beauty operator with all the sweet-smelling creams. The way the roaches go after those lotions!"

Mira, ignoring Lillie du Lac, turned to my mother. "From what Jess told me, I didn't imagine the Angus to be like this. I love old places."

"If you're only going to be here a few days, I have the back room I keep open for the afternoon couple trade."

"Old places make me feel part of something." Mira looked about helplessly to see if anyone grasped what she was trying to say. My mother listened with understanding, Jess with amusement, while Lillie du Lac was annoyed. "I guess I sound silly."

"No, no. I understand," my mother said quickly. "You're like all young people now. You're floundering around in too much space."

Mira looked at Jess helplessly.

"You're doing fine," Jess said. "No one's gotten through to Maw in a hundred and fifty years."

"I'm fifty-nine. Don't make me out any older than I am."

"It's not decent to tell your age like that. It's like undressing in public. If you insist on the Angus being old, that's one thing, but age never made a woman more valuable."

"It's a room off the porch overlooking the huisache tree. The Spanish general kept his mistress there, you know. A lovely girl." My mother couldn't resist selling her rooms even when she didn't want the roomers.

All at once, Sergeant McCane raised his head in surprise and broke the spell.

"The Spanish general was a very virile man," my mother explained.

"And while he was putting his pants back on, Sam Houston walked off with the Republic of Texas."

We all laughed. Even Mira was amused by Lillie du Lac's muddy humor. In fact, after she started working in Lillie's French Sandwich Shop, they got along surprisingly well. Lillie frankly admitted that Mira was the best waitress she ever had, for no matter how cloudy her thoughts, she never messed up on an order. To seal the friendship, Lillie gave Mira a tricky little black and white uniform, and Mira, in a gesture of appreciation, presented her employer with the Polish rooster, which Lillie du Lac called Majenski and kept in a gilded cage she found at the Salvation Army store.

◆ ◆ ◆

The party broke up a little past one o'clock, after coffee and cinnamon rolls in Lillie du Lac's kitchen. I noticed the clock on the Dairy Maid sign and couldn't believe it was so late. I was acutely conscious of precious time passing, yet I tossed it aside like an outmoded garment. Now all I wanted was to get away. I had been part of a crowd for sixteen hours, and I felt a desperate need to stretch out alone. At that point, I regarded this lonely urge rather casually. A whim rather than a necessity. A time to read vaguely from a half-dozen books scattered about my rumpled room and a time to write dreamily in my diary.

We coupled off on the way up the stairs, Jess and Mira staying

THE DUCHESS OF ANGUS ◆ 101

on the balcony overlooking the courtyard. Sergeant McCane fell drunkenly into his room after the hours of quiet saturation. My mother went off to check the rooms for fire and vice, and Lillie du Lac and I walked together down the shadowy hall toward our front rooms. I shivered in the hot night. I could certainly use a warm bath.

"You've never seen my room," Lillie du Lac said. And I knew I would go to bed sticky and caked with blood.

I would prefer to have waited until another time when I was not so exhausted and listless. Now it all seemed pointless.

Lillie didn't turn on the lights. "We can't waken Majenski at this hour," she explained.

But perhaps she was as vain about her room as she was her appearance. I noticed that the neon signs from across the street cast a wonderfully eerie light through the glittering shutters. I knew Lillie du Lac well enough to realize that she hadn't missed this effect. The sparkling shutters were reflected in a great mirror that hung over the bed. She, of course, sensed my interest.

"We grasp at straws around here," she said.

I touched the shutter near me. My God! I thought. She placed the brilliants there while the paint was still wet.

There were hundreds of them. The thought of such tedious labor made me sad. I wanted to cry and at the same time swallow up everything. What crazy games we played!

I sat on the deep windowsill and looked out on the business across the street. Alamo, it was called: the CCM Bar, the Riverside Café, the Saddle Club, the haunts of shabby lushes. A city block from daytime respectability. The high-pitched crowd was being herded out of the bars by the laws of the State of Texas. The only place left to go was the all-night restaurant called the Owl, where great platters were heaped with flat fried foods and carried out on the shoulders of short loud-mouthed waiters.

Someone played the Mexican trotting song. It added a shade of sweetness to all that glare.

"Another damn fool wants to show that he has a nickel," Lillie said, putting her hand on her forehead. "Anyone with a head like mine shouldn't sleep next to a jukebox. Migraines, you know. All I get are the vibrations—the music goes someplace else."

She pulled back the filmy gauze that was draped over the high posts of her bed like a ghostly canopy that hung down on all sides.

"What's that?" I asked.

"Netting, my dear; although there are no flies in San Antonio, there are scorpions and cockroaches. An old trick I learned in the tropics from the Colonel, of course."

"That's what I wanted to talk to you about."

"Not me, certainly. I run from the little creatures. Can't face them. You go to your mama for advice on roaches and such. She meets them on their own ground, looks them square in the eye."

"No, I meant the Colonel."

"The Colonel? What can you tell me about him that I don't already know?"

"But you said I should have lunch with Wade Howell," I pleaded.

"You should have lunch with someone. I won't argue with you there. It's bad for the digestion to eat alone—eat too fast, you know."

"Don't you want to know anything? I thought—" I was on the verge of tears.

"It's a common mistake. You've been fooled by the acoustics around here. They are a joke. Some things echo through the whole place...other times we can't be heard when we shout in each other's ears. The Spanish general was so jealous of his mistress, he wanted to hear her think, but like so many experiments that are not carried far enough—it backfired . . ." Lillie's voice drifted off, and I realized that she had fallen asleep.

I tiptoed to the door. I could have sworn I heard a smothered laugh from inside the mosquito netting. What curious rules was she playing by now? One thing was certain: no matter how well I played, only dumb luck would see me through.

The hall was dark in a frightening closed-in fashion. It had no windows of its own, and when the doors to all the rooms were closed, the walkway perpetrated a shaky feeling of uncertainty. My mother usually kept a twenty-five-watt bulb burning in the back hall, but tonight it was out.

The brilliant crippled engineer who lived in the room next to me always turned it off when he came in drunk, and he came in drunk every night that he didn't get drunk in his room. He had spent most of his life trying to ruin what was left of it. Of course, we all felt sorry for him and never complained when we stubbed our toes in the dark.

I reached over and turned on the switch before going into my room. Then I threw my clothes in a heap and fell diagonally across the bed. I couldn't bear anything to touch me but a clean sheet pulled tight across the mattress. For a moment I was allowed to revel in ecstatic emptiness, until the vice squad crashed into my vague dream. They were picking up some of the more disturbing diners at the Owl. I felt sad and disgusted, and I detested myself for not getting up and writing or reading or at least washing my face. Finally I got up and brushed my teeth. A fat girl in a short dress hiked up in back was dumped into a police car while her saggy-looking date watched stupidly. One push and he fell in after her.

The merry-go-round was slowing down, but the carnival would start up again tomorrow. Curiously enough, my feeling of sadness had departed.

◆ SIX ◆

I woke up late the next morning. It was Easter Sunday and another hot clear day. The sound of church bells made me sweetly melancholy. From my window, I saw the hideously pastel women on their way to church. Beside those animated Easter eggs, the most carelessly dressed men seemed finely tailored. Self-conscious effort would never pass for natural graciousness.

It was quiet in the Angus Hotel. The sounds I heard were the healthy sounds from outside. There was no coughing from parched abused throats or senseless arguing after a night of cheap passion. I listened for a comforting rattle from my mother's kitchen. She must have gone on to church. My uncle's six-month-old baby was to be baptized. "And the Lord knew," as my mother said, "it was high time." His sloppy young wife had postponed it long enough. I wondered if Jess had gone, too. If he thought it would please my mother, he most certainly had. Now I wished I had gone. They might have called me. But I did not expect them to. I had made it plain that I did not care to go with them.

I had created a fragile world of temporary values, and I wanted to keep it alive. Each contact with reality showed it up for the shoddy farce it was. I knew that one day my careful construction would fall to pieces, but I was not ready to have that happen.

My mother was constantly being hurt by what she called my attitude. The trouble was I did not have an attitude. My undisciplined mind danced in an open arena, the most ordinary events taking on a terrible distortion. I felt tongue-tied and incoherent when it came to discussing my activities. The smallest communication seemed like an impossible effort.

I lay down on the bed and looked about my room. The pale blue washed walls rested me. There was no other color in the room but the greens of the various plants that were everywhere: huge rubber leaves that reached almost to the ceiling, tangled ivy vines and fluffy ferns that covered most of one wall, a lone stiff cactus on a white table. My books were in a foot locker under the bed, and a muslin curtain covered the entrance to the closet. This room was every place to me: my home, my cell, my altar, my refuge. I guarded it selfishly. Although my mother kept a pass key at the desk, no one came into my room. Francisco, the Mexican maid, was told to skip it on her morning rounds. "He," as she called me, since she had never learned to distinguish gender pronouns, will clean "his" own room. No one came to the door, and the long bare windows opened onto my world. Lying on my cool bed, I could stay as close or go as far as I chose.

I only had to go as far as last night to indulge in sensual thoughts of Cadet Gerald Eaton. He appealed to me—I had to admit that—but my rambling shambling life appealed to me more. Anyway, I had that. It was doubtful whether I would see Gerald Eaton again. I certainly wasn't going to stalk among ten thousand cadets to track him down. And I had lost his precious photograph in a last-minute struggle for my virginity. How was I going to explain that?

I reached under the bed and came up with my Pre-Shakespearean Drama. I started reading *Gammer Gurton's Needle*, and for fifteen minutes, I took it like a physic. It made me feel good—strong, after a fashion. I was in control of my destiny for a moment. Always reservations, conditions, disturbing interruptions.

If only I could get away from Wade Howell. This thought always troubled me when I was alone in my room. I pulled out a copy of John Stuart Mill as though to tuck that erratic girl between the precise pages of utilitarianism and let her be devoured by reason. I did not need her. I did not thoroughly like her. She didn't bore me, that was true, but the aimless escapades sapped my strength. And above all, there was the burden of gratitude. There was bound to be a forfeit.

Lillie du Lac, in her brief exhaustion and despair, had given me an out. "What can you tell me about the Colonel that I want to hear?" she had said. And she was quite right. What trifling snatches of hearsay could compensate for a lost love? Or perhaps she had come to know me better and like me less and wanted to keep me as far from the Howells as possible. The more I thought about my teasingly fragile relations with the people around me, the more restless and confused I became. I simply had to take a stand.

I finally compromised on a kind of half-martyr, half-counterspy role. For the time being, I would stand by and mark time. If Wade Howell began to infringe on my privacy, which she was bound to do if she began coming to the Angus, I would simply consider it a temporary inconvenience. I promised myself to do this graciously, knowing full well that if I permitted Wade Howell to take over, I would not have the energy or ambition for anything else. She was everything in me that had to be crushed. And would have to be stopped sometime, and if I let it go too far, I might not have the strength. But for the present, I would let go of my hold on the fence and plunge in the deep end and worry about a lifesaver when the time came to go under.

Before the tea dance, I was to meet Wade Howell at the Orangeana, where the tropical drinks taste like bubble bath. The first thing I saw was the back of her neat dark head and the effect of her white dress on the lovely shoulders. I quickly suppressed a pang of jealousy. I hated that mean little emotion above all others.

What curious carnival distortion is this? I wondered.

The resemblance was absolutely frightening. Under ordinary circumstances, no one would need an introduction to know that the woman in the black linen and white fur was Wade Howell's mother. Although this meeting was far from ordinary, since this woman had crashed into an area where she was far from welcome, I got the picture immediately. In the midst of the sloppy Coca-Cola crowd, mother and daughter stood out like a fine-lined pen-and-ink sketch in a window of junk.

"I'm sorry if I kept you waiting," I said.

"This is Jane Davis. My mother."

"Dede dear, get your friend a drink of something." She didn't say *little*, but I felt it.

"No, thank you. I just finished a drink." I did not mention that it was a gin and 7 Up, but one came up and then there were six. Perhaps this pretentious female didn't notice. She had the same icy aloofness in public as her daughter, so it was impossible to tell what penetrated through the glacial layers. Nevertheless I could well imagine her being the rich partner in a shaky marriage that might blow up at any time. Or perhaps her resemblance to a daughter who after three bites of a hot enchilada melted into a veritable puddle of amorality colored my judgment.

"Dede tells me that your mother keeps a hotel."

Keeps indeed, I thought. That goes with the imported linen and slip of useless ermine. All I said was, "Yes."

"It's really darling when you get inside," Wade Howell was saying.

I was slow-witted today, and fourteen hours in bed and gin for breakfast did not make me any brighter. But I did remember that this was the second time Wade had claimed to have been to the Angus.

Suddenly it struck me. Wade Howell was a liar. She lied to impress, she lied to get her own way, but mainly she lied to meet the demand of the moment, which usually amounted to transforming it into a colorful romantic bit of foolishness...which, after all, was no more than anyone with excess energy and a little imagination tried to do, one way or another.

One fact stood out: Wade Howell had not intended for me

to meet her mother. No doubt she had meant for me to be a secret little private interlude, to be jealously guarded from family
scrutiny. But quite suddenly, the gears had shifted and she was
being driven at high speed. I doubted if Wade knew why, but I
felt certain her mother had entered the race.

"But are there cockroaches?" Mrs. Howell asked.

What a trivial woman, I thought. She would not think to ask
me if there was a chance of being raped on the way to the john—
only if there were cockroaches.

"No, I never see any." This was a lie, too, a harmless social
lie for face-saving. I thought very little of it. After all, I couldn't
tell this sterling matron that we entertained what amounted to a
subnation of the detested roaches, and that no one at the Angus
was particularly concerned about the little pests since they had
moved their headquarters from Lillie du Lac's kitchen to the
sweet-smelling dresser drawers of the beautician with a hundred
sweet-smelling lotions. Obviously this woman would never be
acclimated to her environment, since there were always nui-
sances to be overlooked. This city was overrun with cockroaches.
It was part of the charm, like the Mexicans, the soldiers, and
the whores. But as Lillie du Lac always said when she turned on
the light and scattered the roaches, "There are no flies in San
Antone."

"Dede has a notion she'd like to take a room at your mother's
hotel."

There it was. I did not manage to say a few gracious words at
this point, but I guess I managed to look surprised, as though

the idea had never occurred to me. At least this silly woman felt the need to elaborate.

"Dede finds it tires her traveling so far out to the field." Still another kind of lie. This one was also purely social, but of a more positive nature. There was a purpose behind it more personal than a mere desire for amiable social opinion.

"We're very crowded. There are so many army wives." I was stalling for time. The racy game had gotten out of control, and I found a need to check my bearings.

"I'm aware of this. We're army, you know."

I did indeed.

"I'll have to talk to Mother." I could just imagine my mother's reaction. She liked to do business with complete strangers fresh off the street. The shorter the stay, the better. Sometimes she rented a room three times in one night. The best roomers did not so much as turn down the spread.

"It will be nice if you can make it soon."

"I'll do my best."

"Now I'll have to run. I'm meeting friends." And she was off in a matronly bustle of secure self-satisfaction—a truly domestic whore.

I noticed that she was quite short, not more than five feet. Wade was perhaps two inches taller, but those two inches made all the difference. I watched the Colonel's second wife until she was out of sight. Then I turned to Wade. How those two women must hate each other, I thought.

"Thanks," was all Wade Howell said to me.

Thanks for what? I wondered. Like a thief leaving a polite thank-you note. I began to resent Wade Howell in earnest.

◆ ◆ ◆

"The English language has certainly gotten out of hand," I said to Wade, after we had cleared ourselves at the door.

Couples were dancing to a hundred different accents while a five-piece orchestra was playing in pantomime across the ballroom. My raw nerves warned me of the approach of a terribly adolescent-looking cadet. When he came closer, I realized it was Tommy Faraday. Given half a chance, he would have asked me to dance in the hope of being introduced to the unapproachable Wade Howell. Children adored her from afar.

"I hate to appear greedy, but unless I get something to eat, I'll faint." Wade followed me silently as we fought our way to the refreshment table. The committee had outdone themselves.

"If the money spent on clever decorations could be liquidated into the punch bowl, we could have a delicious orgy," I said.

"Sometimes I wonder about you."

"You're lying. You never think about anyone but yourself. But then, lying seems to be a way of life with you." Wade did not hear this. At least she did not let on. I always said nasty things on an empty stomach.

The table was covered with enough white tulle to dress a whole cotillion. The underpinnings were gold satin. Glittering bunnies doing cute things were appliqued here and there. Everything was cute in an extravagant way. A gold chicken was bursting out of a white velvet egg between two silver candelabras. All twenty times life-size.

"That gives me an idea for a prenatal shower. We'll have it at the stadium." I stuffed my mouth and my pockets with cute sandwiches shaped like chickens and bunnies—but too soon. Cadet Gerald Eaton and his friend Swarthout were sitting under a gold arbor covered with white roses. Their shoes were shined, their buckles were polished, and their khakis were pressed. The deviled ham was making me sick, but by the time they got to us, I had managed to swallow it without gagging.

"Let's tear ourselves away from this sticky froth and sink our teeth into some steak," Gerald Eaton said.

"It's against the rules," I said.

"The way you're going after all those dainties, they'll be glad to get rid of you."

"This is Wade Howell, Gerald Eaton and Swarthout."

"Don. The pleasure is all mine," said Swarthout, and he meant it.

"You look married," said Wade.

"I was," said Swarthout, "but she wouldn't dance with me. Will you dance with me?"

Wade Howell would.

"Your girlfriend is a knockout. Swarthout's crazy for knock-outs. His wife was a redheaded knockout, but she had a short memory. Forgot Don before he finished basic."

"He's divorced?"

"Completely—except for the paperwork."

"He seems all right. I mean, the way he's taking it."

"It was a long time ago—three weeks."

"You're cynical."

"I try to please. Let's dance. That pretty cadet will watch the sandwiches."

It was Richard Randolph Atlas III, of course, who was certainly watching the sandwiches—especially the ones I was eating. I waved to him, and he waved back.

The orchestra was playing something we couldn't hear, but it didn't matter. It was too crowded to dance anyway. But everyone was having a good time. A girl with long silver hair was asleep on her partner's shoulder. He looked at her tenderly from time to time, and then looked about at the other girls. Unlike Gerald Eaton and Swarthout, most of the cadets were not so slick in overcoming the rules of the army. They did not get out very often and had to make the most of every minute. Dating an aviation cadet was a rather breathless experience, for they had a wonderfully frantic way about them, as though they were running for a troop train.

Gerald Eaton was not frantic. He did not act as though selective service had quite suddenly tapped him on the shoulder and demanded he come to life. To him, military service was not the big adventure. It was only a small part of the whole, to be endured, at times enjoyed, but always kept in proper perspective.

This, I muttered, is a very enterprising young man.

"I'm twenty-seven."

"Congratulations, I wish I could offer you champagne."

"Relax. I'm only here because I like you."

Wade Howell and Swarthout danced near us. He was better-looking than Gerald Eaton but too blond and sulky for my taste. I enjoyed talkative men who constantly reminded me that they were aware of my presence.

"They look wonderful together," I said.

"You did all right by Swarthout. It takes quite a lot to keep him occupied. He was used to so much."

I felt a sporting desire to exploit Wade Howell's charms.

"There's no adequate preparation for an encounter with Wade Howell."

He grinned at me as though he didn't hear.

"She was the most beautiful redhead I ever saw."

I didn't care for this conversation, but I couldn't let it drop at the point where this fiery redhead had melted us down to common clay.

"I don't care for the color scheme, but I'm sorry for your friend anyway."

"Don't let the sad expression fool you—it's deliberate. It's part of being a thinker. That poor little redhead couldn't go along with his thinking. She was able to put up with everything else... drinking, other women. But when Swarthout started thinking— that was too much."

"It wouldn't bother Wade. She won't even notice."

We had too much time that afternoon to recreate the fleeting spell of the night before. Romance has to be limited or it loses its poignancy. Or perhaps the setting was not right. There was no sawdust in our shoes. Nevertheless, I had to admit that I liked this boy.

"I'm not taking off this uniform until we've licked everyone on the face of the earth."

I looked up from Gerry's bony chest and saw Tommy Faraday baring his soul in a big way to a tiny blond in starched piqué.

"Go back to sleep," Gerry said. "If you're any judge of character, you know that's not me spouting."

I did indeed, but I said, "Aren't you ambitious?"

"Not to save the world. I only want to clean up the country."

Something kept me from laughing. Possibly the gin and little sandwiches.

"If I don't get to the ladies' room soon, you're going to have to clean up the floor."

He laughed. "You're fun. I knew you'd be fun the minute I saw you." He did not really enjoy humor; he merely talked about it. "But I'm serious. As soon as I get out of this thing, I'm going to find a dirty little city out west, hang out my shingle, and see which way it blows. In no time at all, I'll be in politics."

"Where is this political career going to lead you?"

"Who knows?" He hesitated. "I'll tell you one thing—I wouldn't turn down the nomination for president."

"You are ambitious."

"I don't know." He grinned. "It's a limited field."

I had to admit he was right. I didn't know anyone else who intended to be president.

"If you don't waltz me over to the ladies' room, I won't vote for you."

After I vomited, I felt better. A million high-pitched screams greeted me as I came out.

"Just two cadets fighting over a little blond," Gerry explained.

I must have looked like death, for he was all apologies.

"I'm sorry. I'm a heel for not taking better care of you. To hell with the deviled eggs. What you need is some red meat."

◆   ◆   ◆

The four of us had T-bone steaks and french fries in a dark café called the Tropics. Gerry even finagled some whiskey sours by dispatching a silver flask and recipe to the kitchen. It did not matter that they were in champagne glasses, for there was a note tied to each stem hoping we enjoyed our drinks and signed "The Cook." And on one there was a special message wishing the young lady a speedy recovery. Perhaps this boy would be president after all. We could do a lot worse, I thought, and so could I.

On the street in front of the Tropics, I looked at my three green companions. In the ghastly light they looked sick, but I guess I did too. I started to laugh.

"Let us in on the joke," Gerry said.

"I was thinking of us as a composition in color and line."

"That's the funniest thing I ever heard," Swarthout said without a smile. We were natural enemies.

"We missed the bus back to the post."

"I take it back—it's the second funniest."

"There must be some way to get back." I was more concerned than they were. The last thing I wanted was for Gerald Eaton to be restricted to the post for the rest of his stay in San Antonio.

"We'll get a taxi," Gerry said.

"Taxis aren't allowed within three miles of SAACC."

"All taxi drivers caught taking cadets back to camp will be shot first, questioned later," Swarthout read off of an imaginary bulletin board.

"Looks like you had better start walking," Wade said.

"I'd sooner call the Colonel and tell him to get the hell in here and pick us up." This was Cadet Gerald Eaton.

In the end, I went back into the jade-colored café and called a cab while Wade Howell leaned against the stucco wall and watched the two cadets play with the cockroaches on the sidewalk.

By the time I got back, they had decided that Wade and I would ride out with them. Then on the way back the taxi would drop Wade off and then me.

Fort Sam Houston was in another direction, and I could walk home from where we stood. I knew what they were after, and I didn't say a word.

Gerry graciously offered Swarthout and Wade the privacy of the backseat while we sat beside the driver. The long ride seemed all too short. I was too wrapped up in our tender sweet lovemaking to notice what was happening in the back seat. The quiet arguing did not disturb our kisses.

We got to the gates just as the buses from town were unloading. One long goodnight kiss, and our cadets marched stiffly off to war. I got into the back seat. No one noticed the taxi turn around and head back toward the city.

We drove for ten minutes without a word. I had no intention of saying anything. I wanted nothing more from this day but the soft wind on my burning face and the pleasant confusion of my lazy thoughts.

All at once, Wade Howell leaped into the front seat. She had decided to drive. The driver took one look at her and decided it was a good idea. Her driving didn't live up to her walking, which flowed along like a stream, but then she lacked the practice. And, too, there was the distraction of the taxi driver with his left arm thrown casually over her shoulders I had admired earlier and his right arm God knows where.

At one point, we were crashing along the overpass on the Frio City Road as a B-24 came lugging out of Kelly Field, and I felt certain Wade Howell would go to pieces, but she just laughed and drove no hands and we all came out alive. After that, she seemed to get the hang of driving, and we sailed along like everyone else. I was not particularly frightened. I was too full of gin and whiskey and beer for that, but my head ached, my legs twitched, and there was a dull pain in my throat. It annoyed me that Wade would never allow our flimsy escapades to remain pretty but insisted on having them teeter precariously at the edge of the gutter.

We stopped before a deadly little bungalow. If this is the home of the Colonel, I thought, we are certainly carrying the democratic system to extremes. Apparently this was the place, for Wade Howell got out and floated into the darkness.

Running back, she popped her head into the taxi and said, "I forgot to tell you. Gerald Eaton is married. Swarthout told me so."

I was more angry than hurt.

From the doorway she yelled an off-the-shoulder "goodbye" as she was welcomed home by a tall dark man in uniform who curiously enough resembled Gerald Eaton. It was the Colonel, of course. The feeling of heady intoxicating romance overtook me once again, and I was surprised at how little difference Cadet Gerald Eaton's marital status really made.

◆   ◆   ◆

Wade Howell did not come to work the next day. And I had to admit that I missed her. Not that I was anxious for her to come to the Angus. But she had become a definite part of my pattern of living, and the only tangible link with my dazzling yesterday.

There was a storewide After Easter Sale, but without Smarty around shouting obscenities and slapping our fannies when she caught us in a slouch, the Sportshop lost its competitive sparkle. The dirty old girl had known what she was about. "There's more to merchandising than good taste," she always said.

It was at lunchtime that I missed Wade most. We always met in the Fountain Room, carefully choosing a conspicuous table in the secret hope that a lunching executive would notice our pitiful little brown paper bags from home. This, of course, was a conceit in reverse. A kind of whimsy to offset the overall glamour composition we were working on. Usually our sandwiches and cookies were more appealing than anything on the skimpy menu. My mother was an expert with food, and Wade Howell's mother seemed to be a snob about everything—even packing a lunch.

I did not want to sit alone, so I sidled up to two army wives while we waited in line. The bucktoothed Mexican hostess seated us at one table. They were a dreary pair, in their sweaty black dresses flaked with dandruff. Their endless talk of monotonous little doings in miniature makeshift apartments depressed me. In a desperate attempt to escape, I feasted my eyes on the Mexican girl behind the jewelry counter. She was said to be the most beautiful girl in San Antonio—before Wade Howell had come, no doubt. I did not look like that, but at least I had the perception to steer clear of a life of electric plates and bathroom privileges.

By three o'clock I had resigned myself to an uneventful day. Then, in the next half hour, I had three phone calls. The first was from Wade Howell, asking me to meet her at the entrance of the Angus Hotel at eight thirty.

"I've simply got to get away from here," she whispered, "but first I want you to understand that Mother put me up to it in the first place. She really wants to get rid of me, you know. I've got to hang up now—she's coming." I could picture Mrs. Howell standing within earshot. This was probably another of Wade's ghoulish little tricks for getting even with her mother.

The second call was from Mrs. Howell, who wanted to be reassured that her daughter was going to a respectable place. I suspected that the tricks were lost on Mrs. Howell.

The third call was from Gerald Eaton, who wanted to keep in touch.

At the same time that I welcomed the busy confusion, I felt

a stab of regret for the first sweet lonely months of my life in this city that touched me so deeply. I liked the image of my own loneliness. The brief meaningless rendezvous with men quickly forgotten. I promised to keep enough of myself aloof from these new entanglements so that I might go on reveling in that delicious privacy.

PART II

Sometimes I think, well…
and then again, I just don't know.
JESS SAUNDERS

◆ SEVEN ◆

My mother claimed that the Angus Hotel was the third oldest building in the city—next to the Alamo and the Governor's Palace. When she first came to San Antonio, she carried on a sizzling correspondence with the historical society arguing the point. But in the end, she wore them down just as she did everyone else.

The only time she ever lost an argument was when she was battling with the Angelus Funeral Home, and then, she only conceded the point for her own convenience. At that time the hotel was called the Angelus, a name which my mother considered quite appropriate because of the proximity to a cathedral whose bells tolled morning, noon, and night.

"It summons tired wanderers off the streets," she would say to Lillie du Lac when they were sitting over a sentimental beer.

Then it did not matter that mail belonging to the Angelus Funeral Home was delivered to the Angelus Hotel and vice versa. There was nothing very important anyway. But when Jess joined the navy, mail became a very big item indeed. Feelings between the two establishments became strained, particularly on my mother's side. At one point, she openly accused them of keeping a picture postcard of the beach at Waikiki.

It was Lillie du Lac who suggested that my mother get the funeral home to change their name to something else.

"Nobody who goes there cares, anyway," she said.

She even offered them the use of her own name. They refused.

If my mother had not been going out with a man from the slaughterhouse at the time, I think she would have put up with the inconvenience of chasing down her mail rather than lose a battle. But she was quite taken with her butcher, and when he suggested the "Angus" and offered to give her a new sign as a token of affection, she agreed.

The building was old. The outer layer of adobe was dry and brittle. Lately, when there was an unusual ruckus in the streets, portions of the old mud would shake loose and crumble about us. This did not detract from the hotel's appearance. In fact, it became more picturesque after a severe jolt. Hardly a day went by when some amateur artist did not sit under the huisache tree in the back courtyard studying with interest the beautiful ruin.

The courtyard served as our living room and dining room, and, weather permitting, my brother used it as his bedroom. It was enclosed by a jagged wall of careless masonry and furnished with a crazy assortment of discarded chairs and tables. Jess's cot was draped with Mexican serapes, all that he had left of the little housekeeping adventure in Tia Juana. But it was really the perfect balance of the century plant in harmony with the huisache tree that gave the area its feeling of artistic coziness.

The feathery huisache tree reached above the second-floor balcony, lavishing the iron railing, the deep windows, and the massive door with soft shadows. The back door was the main entrance to the Angus Hotel, whose rooms occupied its second story. Just inside and to the left was Mira's room. Across the ten-foot hall was Sergeant McCane's room. My mother had an apartment next to Sergeant McCane, and opposite that was the suite occupied by a beautician and a masseuse. Next to that was a windowless cubbyhole where Jess piled his belongings. Along the front of the building, the hall formed a T. Lillie du Lac, the drunk engineer, and I lived on the short end of the T to the blaring disharmony of the jukeboxes across South Alamo.

On the side of the hall next to Lillie du Lac's room there was a narrow stairway that led to the street and up to the third floor and ten rented rooms. But the doings up there seemed remote and transient compared to our second-story tangle of self-imposed familiarity.

◆　◆　◆

The Monday after Easter, when I came home from work, my mother, Lillie du Lac, Jess, and Mira were preparing for an elaborate meal to celebrate the breakdown of Lillie's diet. We seldom sat down for a real dinner. Usually we wandered haphazardly in and out of Lillie du Lac's kitchen in search of crackers and bits of cheese to go with our beer or cinnamon rolls to go with our coffee. But every few days, we all got hungry at once, and we looked for something to celebrate. Then there followed a great confusion of batter and flour and frying and inspired pinches of first one spice and then another. The orderly monotony of Lillie du Lac's professional cooking gave way to the friendly confusion of a family dinner.

That night it was to be fried chicken and biscuits, and since my mother was an excellent cook, it was a real treat. Even Lillie, who claimed French Creole blood and was from New Orleans, was constantly amazed at my mother's way with food.

Just as we picked up our forks, a trailer truck rolled by on the hot tar, and the Angus Hotel began to deteriorate before our eyes.

"Sometimes I think, well...and then again, I just don't know," Jess said, in such a way that it sounded like a supplication for deliverance. "Well now, ain't that cute?"

And I looked toward the spot that had inspired this remark. This time the outer layer of stucco had fallen off and left a snake-like crack up the side of the wall.

"The pieces are big," my mother said to Jess. "You'll be able to patch that up tomorrow."

"Now, Maw, you know I'm resting up for what's ahead. You never know when something big is coming along, and I don't want to be too tired to recognize it." He picked up one of the pieces and handed it to my mother.

"We'll save the pieces. They might come in handy. We can attach a dirty rhyme and sell them to the soldiers for half a buck apiece—souvenirs, we'll call them." He gave Mira a meaningful look. "Then they won't have to go to the front."

At this, Mira ran up the stairs sobbing into her hands. Halfway up she leaned over the railing and looked longingly at the chicken. Then, in lieu of a handkerchief, she caught up her skirt and went back to her unhappiness.

She not only looks like a cotton picker, I thought, she acts like one. I detested people who allowed straggly ends of emotion to hang loose. Why didn't they tie them up and face the world in one piece?

"I've spent all day mopping up her tears, and now, when we're about to feed her and get her off our hands for the day, you get her started again."

"It burns me up, seeing her mope around after that little cadet."

"Are you in love with her?"

"Steady there, Lillie. You know I can't take kids like that for more than ten minutes at a time."

"I can't understand why he'd go AWOL," my mother said. "He seemed to be a good soldier."

"Tailor-made uniforms and clicks on his heels," Jess said angrily, "that's just what we needed at Pearl Harbor."

"Let's not spoil your mama's good dinner," Lillie said, sopping a biscuit in the creamy gravy.

As for me, I didn't say a word. If I were to mention the fight at the dance, it meant edging in on my privacy, which I clung to as though it were the strongest bough over the abyss of time. The moment passed, and Jess, with his love of harmony, came to the rescue.

"Lillie, how about you and me pooling our resources?" he said. "Your money and experience and my youth and charm."

And suddenly we were back in a game. This one lacked excitement, but it was comforting, because it was so familiar.

"We'll start the sweetest little place down in Panama."

"Watch out there, young fellow, for one of these days when I'm suffering a setback, I may take you up on it."

"It seems to me that there are plenty of bars around here—if you want to be a bartender," my mother said.

"Why, you old hags—I'm not gettin' through to you at all today, am I? You don't think I mean to stand on a catwalk in a dirty old apron...that's not the picture, not at all....What I see is a kind of international oasis that never closes, where every day, just as the sun goes down, ol' Jess Saunders will show up in a white linen suit and a suntanned face, and I'll smile, showing my white teeth, and everyone will wonder what I'm wanted for back in the States."

"If I were a few years younger . . ."

"How old are you, Lillie?"

"That's the darkest secret since the Spanish general hid his señorita's mantilla so she couldn't leave her room," my mother said.

So the play went on. And it was pretense. But only to a point. Like everything else: Lillie du Lac's crazy deuces, a wild gamble for high stakes; Wade Howell's flashy show of precocity in breaking all the rules; my own beginner's-luck hand, played in the vague hope of finding excitement while I waited for one glorious moment of fulfillment; and the marvelous background of war, which we had all waited for so long—the perfect excuse to throw off the gray cape of respectability and play naked among the colored straws—Lillie was only half joking when she said, "If I were a few years younger," just as Jess was only partially telling the truth when he shrugged off the idea of loving Mira, or for that matter of running off to find a cool bar in a hot country. Perhaps our gestures were hazy and inconsequential, but one way or another, we were determined to be caught up in time.

My mother's digs about Lillie du Lac's age were really nothing more than friendly little pricks. The bond of their friendship was deep, and went far back to a time when they were maids together in the home of one of the pioneer families of Fort Worth. If the bond was ever tightened by what seemed like a fantastic turn of an evening's conversation, the union of Jess and Lillie du Lac, I was certain my mother would not be the one to object.

This notion struck me one morning like the splash of icy water before breakfast. As I came into the kitchen, my mother was saying to Lillie, "Jess marrying a nice young girl would be like throwing her to the wolves, for sure. She'd be devoured, and we'd be right back where we are now."

My mother wasn't thinking entirely in terms of finding a safe place for Jess. She considered Lillie du Lac as well. They were two women whose sincere friendship grew out of a long respectful observation of small habits and minute ways. Not that they were alike—although their energetic application to the daily grind suggested it. Apart from that, Lillie appeared frivolous where my mother seemed sensible. If it was the qualities they shared that made Lillie acceptable to my mother, it was the divergence that clinched the friendship. In long-term relationships, there have to be rules to follow, the more complex and intertwined the better, for there is no interest in sameness. Only an illusion of security. And after all, an illusion can be distorted, hidden, or completely wiped out by the ripple of a veil.

It was quite possible that my mother, with her genius for utility, might be sheltering a frail little notion that Lillie du Lac and Jess find more to each other than sparring partners in their daily volley of words. It occurred to me that perhaps my mother was concerned, as well, with diverting her friend from "chasing around after a man," which was a form of "losing your pride." At best, she considered either of these failings as character blemishes, at worst tarnishes, and together they were assassins. Since I had never once heard her bring up the subject of Lillie's hope of flaunting her precarious relationship with her former husband into only Lillie knew what, I assumed that the idea troubled her deeply. All I had to go on was a smile. Not since that Sunday when Wade Howell's picture had come out in the paper had I heard either of them mention the subject. They didn't even talk about it in the intimacy of the early morning kitchen. After all, if a topic can't be discussed before breakfast, when can it? Well, if my mother wished to send two man-eating beasts into the arena at once, knowing full well that she was to be the referee, I would simply close my eyes and turn my head. But of course there were still other beasts in the jungle to reckon with.

Mira came downstairs dry-eyed and hungry. Jess made a great show of clearing a place for her and tucking a napkin in her lap.

No one came close to the testy subject of Cadet Thomas Faraday and his mysterious disappearance. Once again, it was pleasant sitting there in the soft air, sopping biscuits into creamy gravy.

But it was getting late, and Wade Howell was to come at nine. The thought annoyed me. Then, too, I still felt the sting of anger at the cruel way she had told me that Gerald Eaton was married, although by now I had become accustomed to the idea, and was secretly flattered that an attractive married man had found me interesting. How easily we slip from one pose to another!

Even so, at that moment, when I was tired and full and sleepy, I wished I had told her not to come. There must be someplace else she could go to escape the tender tentacles that were driving her insanely in all directions.

In announcing Wade Howell's imminent arrival, I expected indifference or annoyance, but certainly not anger. If I had been less conscious of my own childishness, I might have perceived the same quality recently come to light in Lillie du Lac. Only in the play of love and all its trimmings are we all, like children, in dead earnest. But we never recognize our true likeness in others; we are too intent on fabricating the qualities in them we imagine we ourselves possess. Therefore everything becomes a distortion. And if that isn't enough, we are constantly shifting and rearranging our own characteristics to suit the egoism of the moment. If I had not been swallowed up in my own limited experiences of having fallen into a friendship with Wade Howell and having picked up a few stray men, I would have been more receptive to Lillie's equally childish conduct in establishing, or as I thought hoping to establish, a more binding relationship with her old love. Particularly the night she led me to her room and all but shoved me into her playhouse. But as usual I was a timid rather than reluctant playmate, and my shyness was mistaken for indifference. In the dark, we never found the right toy to establish a common interest. Now I was going to pay for my little deceit.

Suddenly Lillie du Lac threw down her biscuit, dabbed her mouth with a lace handkerchief, and glared at me.

"You and your wild imagination—you've probably colored the Angus to look like a picture postcard," Lillie sputtered in anger.

"On the contrary, I hardly mentioned it. This was Wade's idea, not mine." I felt that I sounded calm, and I was pleased.

"Wade Howell, for God's sake. Why doesn't she stay on the society page where she belongs?"

"You're the one who suggested . . ."

"Suggested what? Three weeks ago, I made an idle remark about having lunch with her, and I hinted that if the subject of my ex-husband came up, I wouldn't be entirely displeased. When two people are married for five years, the relationship is not altogether unhappy, you can be sure of that. A certain attachment is formed that can never be quite severed, even by unpleasantness. I was curious about him, and the meager bits of hearsay he let fall over our coffee were more tantalizing than satisfying. It simply wasn't enough for me, so I began to search for my reflection in the eyes of strangers, but since then, I have been reassured—satisfied—in a most intimate manner. I no longer need the picture since I have the real thing."

Lillie du Lac stormed up the stairs, with Mira close behind making fumbling attempts to comfort her benefactress. Before going inside, Lillie threw this thought over the balcony. "Tell her to stay in her room if she doesn't want to be raped in the hall."

Amusing, I thought.

Also amusing was the curt manner in which Lillie dismissed the disappearance of Mira's young husband, but now, when Lillie was in a panic over what could prove to be at worst an embarrassing situation, her lady-in-waiting was slobbering all over her. Indeed, our system of etiquette was more complex than that of a royal court.

"Sometimes I think, well... and then again, I just don't know," Jess said, lying back on his cot, patting his stomach, and gazing at the stars. I couldn't help but agree.

My mother was more practical. Since there wasn't a vacant room in the house, she suggested that we change the sheets in my room.

"You can share that until something turns up. But make certain she pays half the room rent."

I smiled, thinking this was rather unnecessary advice to give about one so rich as Wade Howell. Anyway, what worried me was being done out of my privacy. I was disgusted with myself for having let it slip away through my own inertia.

◆   ◆   ◆

True to character, Wade Howell arrived on time in two taxis. The first was piled high with dress bags, shoe bags, duffel bags, laundry bags, a sun lamp, a reading lamp, a bed lamp, and two vanity lamps. Wade Howell, among other things, was afraid of the dark. In the back seat of the second taxi, she sat cool and aloof in virginal white. She was holding a flat chest of fine polished wood. Beside the driver of the second taxi was an empty parrot cage, a bundle of old fashion magazines, and a hat box.

I motioned the taxis around to the back so as to avoid using the narrow stairway next to Lillie du Lac's room.

◆　◆　◆

Hours later, I lay on my bed watching Wade Howell in the moonlight. Her wooden chest was open beside her on the windowsill. She was fondling a small object that looked like a bottle, but I couldn't be sure. The glow of the moon, or more accurately the glare of the neon, made it impossible to distinguish a clear-cut outline.

At one point, I heard her say, "I enjoy the night, but I can't be alone in the dark. That's my trouble; I'm always looking for someone to be with when the lights go out."

Although this was a somewhat disturbing thought, I must have dozed off for an instant, for it seemed much later when she asked, "Are you a sound sleeper?"

"Not sound but frequent."

"I hate sound sleepers; my mother is a sound sleeper...or so she says."

There was a pleading note of loneliness in her voice, but I

rolled over on my stomach and put my face in the pillow. For the first time, I was hot in my room, and I felt an unbearable restlessness from which the only escape was sleep. But Wade Howell continued talking.

"The Colonel's different...he likes to roam around at night."

I assumed that she was an insomniac and, like so many others, considered sound sleepers as no better than sloths. On the whole, this misinformed group worried their way through the work day accomplishing little and ending their days in such a neurotic tangle that it was impossible to undo the damage in one night. Like all healthy people, I believed that self-discipline, hard work, and plenty of water could cure most illness. And what those Puritan maxims couldn't accomplish, a good stiff shot of whiskey should. Just before Wade Howell's arrival, I had sneaked into my mother's kitchen and set fire to my nerves. Now I had burned down to a dying ember, and I wanted to go to sleep. But still Wade Howell went on.

"When I have cramps, he comes in and rubs my back. One night not long ago my mother saw him coming out of my room. That's why she's so anxious to get rid of me."

Once again the smoldering fire started to burn, but for the life of me I couldn't decide whether I was jealous of Wade Howell or the Colonel. Perhaps it was the potential of such a lush situation.

All at once, Wade Howell announced that she was going out in the hall to call the Colonel and let him know where she was. My naturally passive nature allowed her to drift into the darkness before I thought of Lillie du Lac's warning to keep her in the room at night. I dismissed this as an angry woman's foolish words.

There was hardly time to regret this flippant conclusion, or place a phone call for that matter, before she was back.

"My mother answered, so I hung up."

When I went to sleep, she was still sitting alone in the moonlight.

❖ EIGHT ❖

Wade Howell took an instant dislike to Lillie du Lac. I was honest enough to admit to myself that this reaction both surprised and disappointed me. We are all matchmakers at heart, of one kind or another. Not that we wish to bring about happiness for its own sake, but there is a minute sense of creativity in displaying friends for the approval of other friends. It is one balm in our great store of potions to relieve the vague but aching desire for greater glory. I had pictured a sweet scene of forgiveness and love.

But who in the world had ever given me the notion that I was any judge of character? I took solace in the small comfort that there was every reason to believe that Wade Howell would like Lillie du Lac. I did not read the signs wrong; it was some kind of inexplicable hoax that anyone might fall for. After all, there was always the obvious: Lillie was an inspired cook and Wade worshiped food; Wade played at amorality whereas with Lillie it was congenital; and above all, Lillie was the natural enemy of the mother whom Wade Howell hated—or so she said. This was all very well to ease my disappointed ego, but the fact remained that alongside of beautiful little Wade Howell, Lillie du Lac was flawlessly commensurable. Admiration inspires jealousy rather than love.

On her first morning at the Angus, Wade reached the bottom of the stairs just as Lillie was coming out of her kitchen. At that moment, I felt my morning trump slip out of my sleeve. Lillie du Lac towered over Wade Howell. I made the introductions, they nodded coolly, and Wade slipped behind her dark glasses.

"I'm going to look for some breakfast," I said, as I settled Wade by the table in the courtyard. And life, true to itself, in the midst of heavy drama came through with a lighter mood. This time in the form of pancakes.

Since before daylight, according to a weepy Mira, my mother and Lillie du Lac had been arguing over the proper consistency of French pancakes. From the looks of the kitchen, the disagreement had progressed well beyond the verbal stage. The thin pancakes were everywhere. There was even one hanging on a geranium in the window.

I went about collecting an even dozen and sprinkled powdered sugar on the fragile perfections. I turned back to the courtyard without a word.

Jess had come down and pulled up a chair opposite Wade Howell. They did not notice me when I came out.

"Doesn't it bother you having that metal next to you?" Wade was saying.

I was aghast. No one had ever dared to openly discuss Jess's

artificial foot. And I didn't even have the nerve to find out if
Wade knew who Lillie du Lac was!

"Not anymore. Not like it used to, anyway. At first it was all
the time gettin' hot and cold around the edges. Now it's melted
down so it feels real cozy in thar."

Wade shivered. "It's senseless."

"Kinda. But so's everything, if you go taking it apart. Take you
being here . . ."

I crashed into the sentence with the plate of pancakes. Their
talk had become much too serious for my taste. A ring of sincerity does not always form a circle, and I wasn't anxious for this
conversation to lead anywhere.

"Lovely," Wade said, finding no cause for argument. She didn't
even ask who made the pancakes.

Jess grinned at me at the same time Wade took off her dark
glasses. I couldn't help but notice her expression of uncontrollable interest as her eyes slipped from blond hair to pale gray eyes,
to tantalizing mouth, to wiry frame and back again. Perhaps
it was that mouth that whispered doom to every woman who
glanced in his direction. It was a passionate, indolent tease of a
form that was all the more inviting because it was kept in firm
control by an intelligent master. Or perhaps the hairline that
grew with such orderly respect around the delectably boned con-
tours of a head that was so flat it was almost concave. Or perhaps
the understated body that never boasted of absurd masculinity
in its undeniable strength. Or perhaps the eyes, clear gray without a fleck of the opaque. So rare, indeed, that it seemed to be

an extravagance to have two alike. Such perfection could not endure.

Temptation ready-made and beautifully wrapped, I read into Wade's thoughts, for one who is used to rolling her own.

Jess was my stepbrother, the one thing I held against my mother. As Lillie du Lac said, "Why on earth, when she had her clamps around that glorious chunk of male, couldn't she have held on long enough to give you that mouth?"

But there was more to Jess than met the eye. By the time he was twelve, he was riding in rodeos and reading naughty novels in three languages. By the time he was seventeen, he was in the navy. By the time he was twenty-one, he had been around the world half a dozen times. And by the time the war started, he was a disabled veteran.

Now, at twenty-four, Jess dragged himself around the little courtyard on one foot while the rest of us went wild with a holiday of adventure. The natural hero sat dreaming in the shade while a million pretenders decked themselves out to take his place.

"Now, Duchess, you wouldn't want us eatin' these here crêpes suzettes without coffee." This semi-illiterate western tone was a pretense and it annoyed me.

"That's right, order me around—I'm just a clown in this circus." I never liked being imposed upon.

"Manners, manners. Remember we have a guest."

This was not at all what I expected. I had imagined Wade swishing through the halls with head high and eyes blank. Her half-whispered incongruous remarks edging unevenly into our easygoing conversations. Jess, once he got over the initial shock of finding her more beautiful than her picture, would, no doubt, find her unbearable. But at the moment, there she sat, a relaxed, sympathetic, and altogether charming companion in my brother's eyes, while I sputtered aimlessly about to keep from being completely overshadowed.

I went to the kitchen for coffee and solace. "At least," I thought, "Lillie will show some spunk after Wade's silent greeting." Instead, there was a bottle of gin on the refectory table, and she was in the midst of one of her vast general reconciliations.

"It's just an act her mother told her to put on," was Lillie's verbal shrug in answer to my prodding. It occurred to me that Lillie was all set to become friends with Wade when she was greeted with a hasty but complete rebuff.

Why all the twist in character? I wondered. A good night's sleep will do wonders, but a night at the Angus was not all that soothing.

"Have some of Lillie's elegant coffee," my mother said. She and her friend were exchanging pancakes and compliments and at the same time tempering the sweet stuff with swigs of gin. This was stretching their irregular habits too far, it seemed to me. Usually they didn't touch anything but beer until after the noon rush. Something had cleared the air, or at least thinned it out.

Mira, on the other hand, was a study in limpness. She resembled a tangled rag doll that a tired playmate had tossed into the corner. Then some whimsical jokester had come along and put a glass of gin in the reluctant hand. The glass was decorated with the usual Mexican figures in bright color and slow motion. I found them fascinating—not for their individuality, certainly, but because the gin had slopped out over the side of the glass and washed the little Mexicans into Mira's lap. Even though she was crying, she struck me as disgustingly funny. Her troubles seemed to lack reality. Perhaps that was the reason I liked her better when she was sad.

"For once you were right," Lillie said to me. "Wade Howell is lovely. The picture didn't do her justice."

I said nothing, but rushed out with the coffee to see why Wade was laughing.

She has a nasty laugh, I thought.

"Don't try to take a bath around here except by appointment," Jess was saying. He was telling her about my mother's bathers from the Labor Temple. It was one of our favorite family jokes, with Jess constantly ribbing my mother for catering to "those two-bit bathers."

"That's the easiest money I make," my mother always said. "They bring their own soap and towels. All I furnish is the water."

After that, we were always wrapped in the comforting humor of the familiar. Wade, too, seemed right at home with this down-to-earth fun.

"Here comes the Duchess now. All we need is some of them finger bowls," Jess said lightly.

"You can dunk your sticky fingers in the rain barrel," I said, with a nasty smile and an edgy voice.

But Jess was not one to go along with a mood. He stifled his

own shrill heartaches with the cruel uproariousness of the professional clown.

"Sis, what's the matter with you? Get out there and entertain
us for a while...kick up your heels...dance up a storm. We've
done et, can't you see?" he said, patting his stomach. "Now it's
time you showed us a little fun. Don't just stand there lookin'
mean—start performin'...name the members of Johnson's
Club."

He turned to Wade. "I'll bet you never knew anyone could do
that. Why, there's some folks don't even know Johnson...God
damn," he said, slapping his leg.

In a way, Jess was complimenting me at the expense of Wade
Howell. But what good was it if she didn't know it?

In the weeks since I had come home, Jess and I had come to
know each other very well indeed. More so, perhaps, than if we
had been together all this time in uninterrupted boredom, for
now we were anxious to make up for lost time. We had been
away, in the tradition of youth, gulping down what the world had
to offer. And in each case, although we came upon the answer
in different ways, the conclusion was the same. All we really had
was ourselves. The idea was to keep a clearheaded open-minded
outlook, stay on the sidelines, and not get pushed along with the
parade. Jess was doing a much better job of following through
than I was, and if he jabbed me with a sharp reminder now
and then, I should feel a consolation in the fact that he hadn't
abandoned me to the hopelessly heavy-handed practitioners of
everyday trivia.

I was ashamed of myself for being so petty. I could trust Jess not to allow himself to appear foolish. Certainly when it came to a woman. In Jess's relations with women, it had always been the other way around.

As Lillie du Lac once remarked about the nights at the Angus, "Until midnight it's the jukeboxes, and after that it's the women falling on their faces tiptoeing in the dark looking for Jess."

I wondered how long before Wade Howell would be groping around in the moonlight counting the doors between our room and his. I couldn't help but feel a vulgar shiver of pleasure. With Mira, Jess was slightly indulgent, like a fond experienced uncle allowing his favorite niece a handicap in the game. Even with Lillie du Lac he would be generous, taking into account her erratic nature. But with Wade Howell, it would be different. They played the game on the same level: point for point and close to the vest.

"She's all there," Jess said, watching Wade slip upstairs. She had eaten five pancakes.

Jess reached under the cot and came up with a battered copy of *Crime and Punishment.*

"You've come a long way in your rehabilitation," I said.

Jess grinned, and we were the best of friends.

◆ ◆ ◆

When we left the hotel for work, I felt a certain relief; I was no longer the hostess. But the moment of peace did not last.

"I like the Angus," Wade said. It was like her not to mention Jess. "And especially our room."

A slash of anger ran diagonally from my left temple to my waist. The truth always had a way of making me unhappy. Was it only yesterday that I was able to say "mine" and not be made a liar by a dozen fancy dress bags? My books were lost in the jumble of equipment it took to keep a glamour girl going. Overnight, my shadowy hideaway had become a torture chamber of light.

The day at the store was more monotonous than usual. Everyone who came into the Sportshop looked like someone who had been there many times before. They weren't buying, and I couldn't care less. I outlined "Andromica" in my sales book behind a rack of Pat Premo dresses. Curiously Wade Howell wasn't waiting for me at lunchtime.

Late in the afternoon I got a call from Mrs. Howell. She seemed terribly disturbed, but only asked if we had managed.

"We managed," I said. I had no intention of giving her any satisfaction.

An impersonal forewarning usually precedes a personal catastrophe. As often as not, the whisper of doom takes the form of a dream or even a shadow. Since misfortune has a way of piling up, it is well to be alert to these hints of destiny if we are to avoid tragedy, which cannot withstand the broad outlook of the perceptive.

As I walked along South Alamo toward the Angus, I was wide open to symbols that might allow me a peek through the crack of doom. An old woman slammed her cracked finger in a car door and her daughter scolded her for being such a nuisance. A Mexican woman snatched her wispy young daughter from the clutches of a group of cadets and proceeded to pound on their flat hats with an old broom.

By the time I reached the Angus, I was certain that doomsday was upon us. A fleet of army jeeps was parked across the front entrance, so instead of going around to the courtyard as usual, my relish for self-torture sent me toward Lillie's French Sandwich Shop, which seemed to be the nerve center of the moment.

A number of photographers had posed a smiling cheerful Mira behind the counter, while an even greater number of reporters were taking down her every word.

"Well, if Tommy hit that cadet, I'm sure he had a reason...if they'd only give him a chance to explain."

"He'll do some explaining all right if they can't get that cut crystal out of the cadet's head."

"You know anything about his family?"

"No, we got married so sudden like, and then Tommy going off to the army like he did . . ."

"It's OK."

"How did you meet Tommy Faraday?"

"I told you. I went out for trick or treat—we were dressed like bums, my girlfriend and me. Then Tommy picked us up and we went out to the highway for some drinks."

"Had you ever seen Tommy Faraday before?"

"Around in school—you know—we never spoke, though."

"How did he happen to pick you up?"

"Just like that—the wind was blowing and he felt sorry or something."

"I'll bet."

"What did you do when he picked you up?"

"I told you—we had some drinks."

"Then what?"

"We talked about getting married."

"And after that?"

"We found us a justice and got married."

"Then what?"

"We got ourselves a motel." With this of all things, Mira blushed.

"Has he seemed upset lately? Bitter with the army—that angle?"

"I can't tell. He doesn't get out much. He doesn't talk much . . ."

"That about wraps it up. Well, buck up, kid—the cadet's not dead yet."

As they began to put away their hot lamps and cameras, I made a break for the kitchen. One of the photographers stopped me and told me how much I resembled the girl on the Dr Pepper sign. I was disgusted with myself for being so pleased. My mother and Lillie du Lac were peeking through the cracks in the partition.

"Poor kid," Lillie said sadly.

"All she ever wanted was a husband," my mother said.

"Poor kid, nothing. She's in her glory." I had become all heated up in the sticky, steamy, sun-drenched dining room.

I joined Sergeant McCane, who was having bourbon, black coffee, crackers, and Roquefort cheese at the refectory table. His bags packed, he had stopped by to have a farewell drink before going on furlough. He was doing justice to his share of the goodbye.

"I never did like that Tommy Faraday," my mother said. "You can't trust anyone who doesn't look you square in the eye."

Even so, I wished that I had danced with him at the Easter party.

◆　◆　◆

My room was crawling with soldiers. They were everywhere. They were under the bed; they were suspended from the ceiling; they were on the ladder halfway up the wall. In reality, there were only three, but crowded as they were with paint buckets, tarpaulins, and beer cans, they seemed like a regiment.

Wade Howell, on the other hand, was set off to advantage on the brilliant white expanse of my bed. She was wearing, of all things, the black and white playsuit that I had sold her before we had become so well acquainted.

At least, I thought, if I'm too late to save my southwest walls from that scorching color, I can snatch my chintz spread from under a certain spray of pink polka dots.

Why, I wondered, did the Goddess of Black and White suddenly switch to pink?

But, of course. My thoughts were so emphatic that it was all I could do to keep from repeating them out loud. The more obvious whores always chose a background of red, or if they wished to appear discreet, they milked it down with white.

But all I said was, "Red…the color of love." That was enough. Suddenly the soldiers began to laugh. Not at what I said necessarily, but merely because they were ready to do something. Wade Howell angrily jerked herself up from the bed and started for the door.

"I'm going out to take a sunbath." It was six o'clock, hardly time for a sunbath—even for Wade Howell.

At the door she turned and said, "I should think you'd be glad to get away from this desolate blue. For once, I agree with mother. Pink at least sheds a rosy light of security."

Her wooden clogs beat a message of anger down the long bare hall. And we laughed until we cried.

"You can't win," one of the soldiers said.

I felt a wave of disappointment. Here I had been congratulating myself on keeping my wits and temper during a trying episode. And what good was it? There was no one to applaud my subtle victory. I looked at each of the soldiers. They were about medium size and the color of sand. I felt certain that had I spent a lifetime with them and never seen another soul, I would not learn to distinguish one from the others.

"Army brats," one of them said, "they're all alike."

"Who told you to come here?" I asked.

"The Colonel's wife."

"What's he like?"

"Colonel Howell? He's a swell guy. Not much on the ball. But why should he worry as long as he has the army and the women?"

"Like they say—behind every great man lies a woman, but Colonel Howell lies between two."

And the far-off dreams and vague yearnings persisted.

◆   ◆   ◆

There is nothing so stimulating as the misfortune of others, providing it's not too remote to touch our limited imaginations nor so close as to render us incapacitated by emotional stress. Mira's unfortunate marriage was a perfect target for unlimited speculation. Then, too, her ghastly happiness in the face of disaster, and the fact that she had gone off with the sheriff "to get away from the publicity," enlarged the subject considerably.

"Getting away from publicity, indeed," my mother said. "Trailing after it is more like it."

We scattered about the courtyard after a lively meal of enchiladas and beer. Jess and Wade Howell were sitting on the bench under the huisache tree. My mother, Lillie du Lac, and I were around the table. Early in the meal, I made the usual decision to cut my class in Pre-Shakespearean Drama. I soothed my aching conscience with the now exhausted excuse that enchiladas was my favorite dish, and it took time to appreciate its uninhibited flavor.

In order to prove this point to myself, I began to concentrate on flavor. I stared at the spot on the wall where once Tommy Faraday had sat in silence, looking over his shoulder. Was it possible that was only three nights ago? Now there were crickets crawling around on the broken rock.

"Have you noticed that all the bugs in this city crawl about,

leaving the soft air free to lull us into a stupefying drowsiness?"
I said.

At that moment, I was madly in love with the time and the
place...and let the people go hang.

"I'm cutting my class tonight."

"After that speech, I'd say you'd better," Jess said.

We soon became slightly bored with the subject of Mira, but
we went on with the repetitious conversation and talked without
listening.

"That little gal was sure happy about being married to a criminal," Jess remarked.

"All I can say is it's a peculiar way to act."

"Not at all, Duchess. She was just being herself." This was as
strong a rebuke as I had ever heard Jess make. I hadn't realized
he was so fond of Mira.

"That's the one thing I'll never be able to forgive her for,"
Lillie du Lac said. "I've had her on my hands for two days—
paying her, mind you—while all she did was cry all over the or-
ders...and him roaming around the city picking up women and
knocking down men."

At that point, Jess went a little soft. "You can't hold that against
her. Gettin' a husband was what the little girl set out to do. But she
has to know where he is, otherwise she don't believe she has one."

"She knows now, all right."

"And she's happy."

"I never saw anyone so happy."

"Sure she's happy. No one ever paid any attention to her

before. Oh, maybe a little handout here and there. But now she's the center of things. She's married to someone important. And on top of that, everyone knows it."

"I heard the cadet's improved."

"Well, that's something at least."

At that point, I thought I detected a general note of forgiveness. Since afternoon, rationalization had set in and had time to rip through the clean initial impression and left each of us in an individual murky comfortableness. Nothing remains in focus long enough to form a clear picture. Bits of this and that creep in: a crushed insect in one last painful wiggle, particles of dust from yesterday's careless cleaning, stale tobacco from the pocket of an old suit. The daily mess that animates the dancing dolls.

Mira's smallness was a vivid reminder of our own shortcomings. To pass judgment on her silly self-centered actions was to deny all the trivia that went to make up what we called "life." I, for one, was not ready to do this. There was no substitute. Despite its little nastiness, life was dear. How many bright shiny moments are there, anyway? Mira would be welcomed back without question.

No telling how long we might have sat there lopping up beer if Lillie du Lac had not let slip a thoughtless remark that upset Wade Howell.

"Don't you have an opinion—like everyone else?"

Wade replied with her most effective weapon: a silent walk up the stairs and out of sight.

"Sometimes it all seems so pointless," I said.

Lillie du Lac turned angrily in my direction. "You're the worst of the lot," she said. "At least they keep up some pretense."

My mother and I picked up the dirty dishes together and carried them to the kitchen. It was useless to say anything to Lillie du Lac. She was a child who said the first thing that popped into her head.

♦   ♦   ♦

Later, in our room, I found Wade Howell wriggling into a tight black dress. A white collar gave it a touch of innocence.

"I'm going for a walk," she announced, with chilly gaiety. Lillie's remark apparently had more effect on her than she would have me believe.

"It's ten thirty," I said, hoping she would elaborate on her plans.

"I like to walk at night," was all she said.

I spent an hour flipping listlessly back and forth between Shelley and William Dean Howells. Then, in desperation, I raced madly through Dos Passos. It was no use. The smell of paint made me nauseous. I turned off a dozen lamps and started for the balcony. As I walked through the shadowy hall, I found sullen pleasure in the dim thought that Wade Howell would return to a dark room. After all, she hadn't reminded me to leave a light burning.

For a time, stretched out on an old velvet sofa, I luxuriated in solitude. I thought of Gerald Eaton and experienced a moment of panic. Perhaps I had reached the point where I was doomed to accept flimsy relations with men whose lives were such a complex of thoughtless entanglements that they could offer me nothing more. Here I was, almost twenty-one, and no one had seriously proposed to me. And worse... I was still a virgin.

The soft air, the lacy silhouette of the huisache tree, and the smoky smell of tortillas were unobtrusive reminders that life zigzagged on its own crazy, hilarious, wonderful, sad, happy way. And once again I felt the sweet sad promise of the city I loved.

But I must have fallen asleep, for I woke up to the pounding of enemy soldiers at my bedroom door. They were checking to make sure that every room was painted pink. It was strange how often I dreamed of our enemy in those days, for I rarely thought of the war in the daytime. It was an encouraging sign, I thought, that rather than assert the harsh character for which they were famous, they were always subordinate to the all-over scheme at the Angus, and they seemed content to perform quite trivial tasks in a gentle although unhumorous manner. Our own soldiers, on the other hand, always appeared as clowns in a worldwide circus.

A light wind was banging the screen door open and closed. Coming out of my senseless daze, I could have sworn I heard someone making love in the courtyard below. It struck me that it might have been Jess and Wade Howell. No matter how fantastic the dream, it never came up to reality.

By the time I walked back to the short end of the T, I was fully awake. Going down the front stairs was a familiar lean loose figure. I stood at the door a moment, shivering in the heat. It was

Gerry Eaton. But that was fantastic. Cadets weren't allowed out after ten. Less fantastic, to my tired self-esteem, was the dim but soothing emergency recollection of the resemblance between Gerry Eaton and the man who had greeted Wade at the door of the little white house on the army post. After all, it was possible that the Colonel was coming to see Lillie du Lac. Her sudden loss of interest in talking about him bore that out.

Wade Howell was asleep when I came in. At least she pretended to be. At any rate, there had hardly been time for her to run from the courtyard around the Angus, undress, and get into bed. I lay down beside her. Only then did I realize that I no longer smelled paint. In its place was a new smell, new at least to my room. I had changed enough dirty linen at the Angus to recognize the inimitable odor of love.

◆ NINE ◆

The following Saturday I had lunch with Richard Randolph Atlas III. The idea occurred to me as I lay hot and sleepless beside the relaxed, foul-smelling Wade Howell.

My barren windswept corner was no longer an inspiration to me. I spent as little time there as possible. Where it had once rejuvenated me, it now stifled me. The disgusting confusion of senseless paraphernalia, the sticky sweet-smelling cosmetics, and someone else on my cool smooth bed. That was the worst—the loss of those luxurious hours in bed alone. Now, each time Wade rolled over, I moved closer to the wall. Until late at night, my once dim room was ablaze with light. There was no place for me to rest. I often wondered what it would be like if Wade were a man. Would I ever be able to tolerate the demands of a lover?

Tonight, in my restlessness, this thought got me out of bed. I sat on the windowsill and studied Wade's peaceful silhouette. Passions spent. Completely abandoned to sensuous sleep. Her experience must certainly have been satisfying to have caused this fastidious creature to toss aside all pretense of hygiene. I could hardly contain my curiosity. I wanted to wake her up and demand to know all. But what would I say? "I saw a shadow on the stairs and the odor of love is keeping me awake." Once again I cursed the timid, subdued nature that held me back.

In the morning she would appear scrubbed and poised and fetchingly sad. Our misty relationship was not of the nature to bring forth intimate confessions. Neither of us had the capacity for deep friendship, and we were worlds apart in experience.

I sat motionless. Never had I felt so completely incapable of physical exertion. Yet my whirling dizzy thoughts were slamming me about to the point of violence. It was as though I were suddenly in another atmosphere, and I was unattuned to a more rapid passing of time. My thoughts were fragmentary and undefinable. It was only later that it occurred to me, and I was rather amused at the thought, that it was clearly symbolic of our mood of transiency in those days that I should be completely jarred to pieces by a vague suspicion of Wade Howell having an affair with Gerald Eaton, whereas the altogether probable knowledge that he was married seemed to hardly warrant the superficial gesture of lighting an extra cigarette.

Well, if this advanced game of lust were so much more satisfying than the occasional game of knees which I endured, perhaps I should look into it. As things were, I felt left out.

It was then that I thought of Dick. It was funny that he came to mind, for I had never felt any desire there beyond the touch of his lips on my hair. Perhaps it was because he was so clean. Since I was going about this so clinically, I might as well be practical.

The brief breezy note I wrote to Dick gave no hint of my mood. I asked him to meet me at Frenchie's Black Cat Café, a clattering twenty-four-hour slop house with the most inclusive menu in the city. It was half a block from Joske's. And next to the Gunter Hotel, it was the most famous landmark in the area. The cadets could never be trusted to find the Alamo. I signed my name with a flourish, climbed over Wade, and went to sleep.

◆   ◆   ◆

It was like Dick not to answer.

"There are some things you should know," he always said.

I knew he would meet me. For four days, my thoughts were a kind of self-centered theater in the round, sluggishly occupied with well-rehearsed scenes of our reunion. They were all very tender, and we always parted with an understanding. This was ridiculous. I was trying to dream up a romance because my passions were aroused by someone else's love affairs. I kept telling myself that Wade Howell's sordid romances with lusty phantoms disgusted me, when in reality they had intensified my little fleck of jealousy to the point of actual physical pain.

On Saturday I asked for two hours at lunch. I intended to surrender myself completely to Richard Randolph Atlas III, and an hour seemed such an abrupt calculation of time in which to lose one's virginity.

By the time I got to Frenchie's, a group of Mexican girls were giggling and pointing to the handsome cadet with the picnic basket. Dick did not notice.

"We can spread ourselves out under a palm tree by the river," he said.

This fit in perfectly with my plans. I must have been nervous, for I couldn't remember what I had planned to say.

Instead I said, "Where did you get the lunch?" Which was not at all the tone I wished to set. I began to wonder whether two hours would be long enough.

"I've been on KP. The cook was a swell fellow and let me raid the refrigerator."

Whether or not the cook was a "swell fellow," Dick certainly was. Everyone liked him. He should be the one aspiring to a political career, I thought. I suspected he lacked imagination, or rather perception. He was still very young, so he must have possessed the former. That, possibly, was why I appealed to him. Perhaps I should try for this one, who was barely engaged, and play the fast game with someone else.

"Good God!" I thought, "why do they have to make it so hard for us?" All this pretense of being something better or at least something different than we are. Really, when you get right down to it, they all wanted an experienced virgin.

The lunch itself was delightful. And, of course, furnished as it was by the army, it was generous. There were deviled ham sandwiches and deviled eggs. Very appropriate, I thought, on the day I'd chosen to go to hell. Dick had thoughtfully wrapped a bottle of Rhine wine in a sopping wet towel. The combination of wine, sun, and food made me so sleepy that I thought seriously of postponing the seduction. Then, suddenly, I came to life.

"This is my last time out. We're being transferred on Monday."

I was surprised that I felt so sad.

"Why didn't you tell me sooner?"

"You're always rushing madly from one date to another."

This was true. If I had spent more time with this sweet boy, what I was about to suggest would not seem so abrupt.

"I'm sorry."

"But I'll write to you. I won't forget you."

No, I thought, perhaps you won't.

It was not hard to find a secluded spot among the tangled shrubbery. For the duration of the war and the manpower short-age, the Daughters of the Trail Drivers had undertaken the task of pruning and landscaping along the river. Apparently they intended letting the foliage revert back to the previous uninhib-ited state it had enjoyed when their ancestors stalked the prairie.

I pretended exhaustion, and Dick tenderly made a place for us under a leaning vine-covered tree trunk that had been uprooted by a recent freak storm. He was not much of a naturalist, for the luscious vine proved to be poison ivy. At the time, I was too pre-occupied with the tight schedule ahead of me to be concerned with the world about me.

"I'm going to miss you, little girl," he breathed into my ear. "I've pretended not to care, but you've been tearing me apart."

This was going to be easier than I thought. In no time at all his lips had traveled to my throat. They would have gone farther if I hadn't raised them to mine in a wide-open kiss. Then for a moment we separated and looked at each other with flaring nostrils and drooping eyelids, the pose of passion. In no time we were tumbling in the vines. My skirt was up around my neck. I felt Dick pressing against me, and I slipped my legs around him. Then suddenly he tore away.

"I can't do this to you," he said. "Some guy is going to want to marry you."

It's a helluva time to start a classification system, I thought.

I stood up and brushed down my skirt. Mumbling something about having to get back to the store, I headed toward the Angus. I was in no condition to work.

As I started up the stairs to the street, I thought I heard Dick say that he loved me, but I couldn't be sure. Now I would never know, for I was in a dangerous state of suspension and I couldn't stop. Not that it mattered much. I had no terribly compulsive feelings about him. But I did like to check things off in neat little categories. Anyway, the lunch had been good.

◆ ◆ ◆

At this point there was nothing I wanted so much as to be alone in my room. Pushing my way through the hot crowds, I thought of the breeze blowing the clean white curtains on the tall windows. I began to itch.

Almost everyone who stopped at the Angus came through the courtyard. The entrance on the South Alamo side was nothing more than a narrow opening and a steep dark stairway. Originally this had been the only opening in a block-long adobe wall. My mother always claimed that if the Battle of the Alamo had been fought here instead of down the street, things might have been different. My mother had an odd mixture of sentiment and cynicism.

In later years, when the ground floor of the building had been chopped up into tiny stores with glass fronts, the wall lost the look of Spanish seclusion. But despite the sidewalks, crowds, buses, and neon, it was the original wall that seemed to belong. In the blinding sun, when the glare of the glass was unbearable, the dull walls were a cool relief. Silhouetted against the night sky, the massive wall was a powerful composition, while the neon swam off into the night in a wild blur.

Once, when my mother first came to the hotel, an old man had a heart attack at the top of the stairs. Lillie du Lac had discovered his body on her way to prepare breakfast.

"Martha," she had shouted, "fill the scrub bucket with essence of pine. Someone pissed out at the bottom of the stairs."

After that my mother had made a sign from an old laundry box and nailed it to the front door. "Rear" it read, and there was an arrow pointing in the direction of Houston Street, Austin, Dallas, and Canada. As far as we knew, no one ever took the arrow seriously. Enough tired transients had understood that it meant to turn right at the end of the block to have made the Angus Hotel a lively business.

Now only a few of us used the stairway on South Alamo, and then only once in a while. It was much more pleasant to linger in the shady courtyard before climbing upstairs. So, of course, I was startled to brush up against someone in the narrow darkness. By the time I reached the hall above, two rather flimsy impressions had merged into a spasm of recognition: I had encountered a fat man on the stairs. I looked down and waited for him to open the door. A bald head and a silver bird glowed in the sunlight.

I was wild. A friend of the family no doubt had come to straighten out the incorrigible Wade Howell. That meant she was in my room, and I so desperately wanted to be alone.

Even our most fantastic mental meanderings never take the turns that would brace us for the inevitable confrontation with reality. A lobster-red Lillie du Lac, glazed in anger, stood against the white and gold glitter of her room at the top of the stairs. She was wrapped in half a dozen white Turkish towels and was apparently waiting for me. But I was supposed to be working.

"I don't imagine it ever occurred to you that I might want to be warned of his coming."

Instead of grounding me, this sent me off to the flimsy realm of my own half-formed notions of the mystery of life. It occurred to me that I had never visualized Judgment Day as anything but cloudy and overcast. Certainly none of this bright dizzy heat. A comforting view that left us pretty much immune to any final reckoning. But then we were on a holiday...the Celebration of Moments.

"You know as well as I that I give myself a treatment on Saturday afternoon." That much was true. Everyone knew Lillie closed early on Saturday in order to "put the tingle back in the old hide," as she put it. This was accomplished through a torturous ritual of ice-cold towels.

"They sent the Colonel here, I'm sure of that."

Only then did I bounce back to earth. If it was the Colonel I had bumped elbows with on the stairway, who was the tall thin man who resembled Gerry Eaton? My spirits kicked up in an uncontrollable jig of joy. In my determination to retain my holiday happiness, I not only grasped at straws, I twisted the brittle shreds in all directions. If they did not snap in my face, it was only because I turned my head in time. It seemed altogether possible that Wade Howell was having an affair with the dark man in the doorway of the little white house. And in that case, Gerry Eaton was left to me. At least for now. I didn't mind that he was married or that I had made such a fool of myself with Richard Randolph Atlas III.

"You always pick the damnedest times to smile. Will you take that shitty grin off your face and come on in?"

I realized then that Lillie du Lac was not angry at me but at the circumstances that had brought her ex-husband to her room at an inopportune time. It was possible that this would upset Lillie du Lac, who was never one to approach even the most trivial event without thoughtful care. And to let a major crisis slip by without tedious preparation was unthinkable. I had happened along at the right time to serve as a convenient whipping boy for her thwarted ego. But in my present mood, I could afford to be generous.

"I'm sorry," I said.

"Maybe you are, even though you don't look it."

"I'm really sorry," I repeated, "and if there's anything I can

do to help . . ." That was quite possibly the most insincere combination of words that ever hit the air, and in the next instant,
they not only exploded but the blinding residue was blown back
in my face.

"Do?" Lillie du Lac screamed, throwing a wet towel at a gilt
mirror that reflected the blinding midday sun. "There's nothing
to do but sit back and despise myself." And the ice-cold towel
cracked the red-hot mirror in eight pie-shaped pieces. Lillie du
Lac was frantic. She ripped a pleated dust ruffle from the bed,
wadded the mosquito netting into a ball and threw it into a corner with the wet towels. And with a silver hairbrush, she began
beating out a savage rhythm on the marble-top dresser. But even
her rage was conducted with efficiency. The electric clock, which
was the only harsh note of practicality in the room, reminded
me that hardly two minutes had passed since I came in from the
hall.

"I'll tell you what you can do; you can get that girl out of here."
One by one, the towels had worked their way off. Lillie was quite
naked, dashing about with her stiff hair sticking out in all directions. I was standing by the door now with my back to her,
trying not to notice her nakedness, but even so I sensed that she
possessed a certain style, like an animated sphinx.

"As long as you've decided not to work this afternoon, you
might as well get started on her immediately."

If Lillie du Lac had not made this presumptuous little observation, I might have gone along with her. But as it was, I resented
her intrusion into my shallow affairs, and I momentarily allied

myself with Wade Howell's shaky position. I pretended, almost to my satisfaction, that I had no idea why the Colonel turned up when he did. The hoard of admiration that Wade Howell had built up in my mind paid off. I would not admit, despite her insinuations, that she had enticed her stepfather to her room—at least not merely to flaunt her sordid affair in front of Lillie du Lac. It was one thing to rebel against her mother, who was a natural enemy, but Lillie was someone to be revered.

Oddly enough, I wasn't doing anything of the kind. But then what could she expect when she let all pretense slip to the floor? One thing was certain. As much as I wanted my room to myself, I was not going to cause Wade Howell to leave unless I had a reason of my own—one I could live with. For little by little I had come to understand the terrible greed with which we guard the least little facet of our pitiful lives. I was clinging to Wade Howell in desperate secrecy despite the fact that she changed the color of my room, took up more than her share of the bed, and perhaps was having an affair with my current flame, although at the moment, the mere possibility that she was not was enough to sustain me. The face-saving loopholes of shallow pride form an intricate maze that would confound the brilliant.

When I opened the door to the room, Wade Howell was standing before the mirror in a flimsy white robe. Except for an occasional dash of a scarf or glint of a bracelet, there was nothing in her wardrobe that was not either black or white. She slammed shut her wooden chest, locked it, and turned to face me. The transparent covering reached out for me in weird supplication, while the familiar bronze body stood stiff with the wind at its back. She flaunted herself as though the female form were something peculiarly hers.

The bed was rumpled and spotted, her tan face was flushed, and the white breasts showed signs of having been fondled. It annoyed me that I felt sodden and rumpled in the presence of this nasty little goddess of sex.

"Checking the family jewels?" I asked, and then felt silly.

She half sniffed, half spoke a crooked little sound. "I was trying to improve myself," I thought she said, and I didn't feel so silly.

"You'd have a lot more privacy in the big corner room upstairs," I started to say. Then I checked myself, realizing it was a hopeless suggestion. As long as she continued to stay at the Angus, I knew there was no hope of being to myself.

"I have nothing to hide." She bore this out in one of her wonderfully feline movements, which swept over my little bridge of scorn, anger, and disgust, at the same time slipping out of her fragile covering and standing naked before me in contempt of any ordinary rules of conduct. This indeed was a bright hot day for exposure.

"Do you like what you see?" She looked past me to the giddy view from our window.

It was four o'clock by the clock in the Blue Bonnet Laundry. The white-hot buildings began to exude the heat they had soaked up all day. She looked out on the Owl, the Riverside Café, and the dirty windows of the CCM Bar. Her expression of sweet sadness bore no relation to her greedy remark and devouring action, and for a moment, I was mellowed by the recurrent mixture of pity and awe, which if not arrested by Wade's flickering moods, might naturally have jelled into a tender mold.

But she turned to me with opaque eyes and a haughty expression, and I felt the insignificant but nagging dislike reserved for a master. Our roles had been cast from the beginning. If we switched parts now, it would only result in chaos. Wade Howell was in the lead and I was under her spell.

"I feel wonderful," she said, striking up a languid pose. "Give me an old man on a hot afternoon anytime."

She paused a moment, picked up her robe, and peeked through a filmy corner to see what effect her remark was having. I turned to the washbasin and started brushing my teeth. The last thing I wanted was to expose my intense flattering interest. Thank goodness she took no offense and continued with her curious ramblings.

"They stay cool and composed and don't spill out all over me."

I was beginning to spit blood, but I went right on massaging my tender gums. After all, I had apparently hit upon exactly the right mood, and I had no intention of breaking into this fascinating flow of words if it meant bleeding to death.

"Mother, the silly thing, sent him in here to check on me. She doesn't know we've been doing it for years."

I braced myself against the basin and spit out the last mouthful of pink peppermint foam before turning to Wade Howell. She was sitting on the windowsill hugging her knees. Her expression hadn't changed, except that the mouth seemed a little less

certain and the eyes a little more hollow than usual. But her attitude suggested the exaggerated schoolgirl confidences shared in
cold virginal dormitories on a quiet Sunday night. Was it possible
to be so coolly calculating? I stood shivering in the sun. Looking
out on South Alamo, I was thankful for the bright heat and the
insane business below. Only when I opened the door to escape
into the hall did it strike me that I had not said one word during
Wade Howell's devastating striptease.

"It's a shame your friend had to see him leave. I suspect she's
still in love with him. But then people never know when to keep
their doors closed."

I closed our door rather hard and stood blinking for a moment, trying to get used to the soft darkness. It was a relief to
see my mother pointing a scissors at one of the roomers. Even
though I didn't relish the idea of her seeing me loll about the
Angus when I should have been working. The only time I was
embarrassed about my sluggish attitude toward my job was when
I was confronted with the actual physical spectacle of my mother
enthusiastically going about her business. Now she was easing
one of her "guests," as she called them, out the back door.

"You don't catch me sitting around waiting for a pension."

She emphasized her point with the point of the scissors. The
poor little old veteran eased his way to the stairs. But she hadn't
finished with him.

"And another thing—all those newspapers you've got stacked
up in there, a fire hazard if I ever saw one. And that's not just my
opinion—the fire inspector has something to say about that."

That put fight back into the old soldier. If there was anything still worth a battle, it was the neat stacks of yellowed newspapers piled from floor to ceiling in his third-floor room. He pushed the scissors aside, stood up straight, and tried to push past my mother. His regular five o'clock supper would have to wait. He had no intention of leaving his precious plunder in easy reach of the enemy. But the sweet little man didn't stand a chance against a foe who was armed to the teeth. And I mean literally! My mother would have made an excellent burglar. She went about the halls with long needles or nails between her teeth and secret weapons concealed in slim pockets, invisible loops, and graceful folds. She weighted herself down in the name of efficiency, and although I'd never seen her jab that torturous hardware into any of the roomers, I am quite certain that the idea occurred, if not to her, at least to them. The people who lived at the Angus had a great deal of respect for my mother and her knives and skeleton keys and essence of pine. She kept order, neatness, and, most unusual, an atmosphere of hopefulness in a cheap hotel.

The little soldier realized he wasn't going to break past the barrier, so he reached in his pocket and handed over the week's rent. He did this quickly and in the exact amount. I guessed it was all he had. Well, Jess would be good for a meal or two. And as my mother said, "Business is business."

I answered the phone from the extension in the hall. It was Mrs. Howell. I had come to expect her call every day at Joske's, but today, since I was at home, I had forgotten all about it.

"I called Joske's, but the girl at the desk said you must have taken sick and gone on home."

Joske's in their big broad way seemed to accept my spasmodic illnesses as a symbol of the times. I didn't object to Mrs. Howell's having called attention to my absence, nor did I object to her frequent phone calls anymore. At first, when I considered her an oversolicitous mother, I was closemouthed, hoping by my suspicious manner to plant uneasiness where I pictured nothing but luxurious bliss. But lately, as I began to suspect that she had something to be anxious about, I assumed an airy tone of girlish enthusiasm. One thing I neglected to do was to credit her with any intelligence. No one with a doll face and a plump figure, I decided early in our relationship, could be expected to think.

When she said, "Can you be here in an hour? There is something I can't say on the phone," I answered yes without thinking.

It was only when she began a carefully worked-out plan to get me past the gates of the army field that I had visions of cool showers and freshly pressed clothes. Then I became rather hesitant.

"Something's happened to Wade," she said, with breathless desperation.

I went back to my eager girl's-school tone.

"No," I answered, with a certain degree of assurance. I honestly didn't believe anything could possibly happen to Wade Howell.

To avoid the two snarling clawing beasts, I used the bathroom in the hall and slipped out the back door. In less than half an hour, I had washed my face and shaken out my pale blue dress, and I was off on another rollicking bus ride through the scorching streets. Going north, the bus was called "Army Post," but it would take more than a flick of the wrist to grind out its southbound character. As far as I was concerned, it was "Nogalitos" in any direction.

My slight concern gave way to hopeless unconcern when a beautiful, filthy little Mexican with a grape sucker and a toothless cowpoke with a mouthful of tobacco slime formed an unbeatable conspiracy against my fading Easter linen. I took comfort in one of Jess's dictums: "Clothes are like a railroad ticket; the more you pay, the farther you go." It was a cheap dress, but I couldn't resist that tempting blue color under the hot sun. And in a short week we'd gone a long way together.

The boy and the man got off among the rutted streets and narrow shacks, and I settled back in an attitude of strained anticipation. Although I had seen the neat little bungalow where I was to meet the Colonel's lady, my imagination refused to focus on it. Instead, it kept shifting to a more pretentious setting of cool white walls and bright Indian rugs, where we sat on high-backed mission chairs surrounded by acres of stucco and flagstone. I could always trust my fancy to place me in appropriate settings of exquisite taste. As it turned out, the Colonel's house was neither of these.

A khaki-colored limousine chauffeured by a PFC to match picked me up at the entrance of Fort Sam Houston. By the time he deposited me in front of the house, I was so completely torn up with emotions of one kind or another that I was unable to articulate even a simple protest. Then I saw a "Colonel Howell" sign the size of a "Keep Off the Grass." I was relieved, if only for a moment, to be able to stand alone in such important shade and study the redbrick horror in front of me.

Even so, I thought, that's more like it.

Taken geographically, this edifice of monstrous gloom was all wrong, but socially it rang exactly the right note of seedy elegance to catch the limited pitch of a colonel in the army.

Mrs. Howell, in pink chambray and diamonds, was waiting for me on the front porch. Over and above everything else, she succeeded in looking rich.

"I'm delighted you felt free to come," she said.

Neat, I thought. Why doesn't she announce that the emotion of the day will be delight?

I said nothing. It annoyed me that from her point of view, she had gotten way down to the fine points, whereas she had not even given me time to change my dress or check my emotions.

But the lady was no housekeeper. Here was tangible proof of the popular generalization that navy men have the ugliest women and army men have the worst housekeepers. For as she led me through the dusty oak hall, I noticed that all the family junk had not been moved to my meager room after all. The Colonel's blouse on the back of a chair was the most cheerful thing in sight. I had an impulse to salute it.

"The army keeps us on the move," she said, of three footlockers.

"Is Colonel Howell being transferred?"

And for one stunning moment, I saw Colonel Howell swept away in a vast entourage of trunks, lamps, and laundry bags, with Mrs. Howell at the top of the heap triumphantly shouting commands and waving goodbye to the tiny breathless figures of Wade Howell and Lillie du Lac running behind.

"My dear, would you believe it, I haven't unpacked from the last move."

And once again, I lost all sympathy for this silly woman.

"The house is completely inadequate. No place to store."

She was not embarrassed by what I considered inexcusable slovenliness. In fact, she seemed quite pleased with this frivolous picture of herself not being able to cope with the lack of space in a house that had at least twelve rooms. My mother would have turned this establishment into a going business in twenty-four hours. This amused me, and I smiled. Mrs. Howell noticed.

"Do we seem strange to you?" she asked.

In a breath, she had inflated our limp wartime social scene to the bursting point.

She can't really be as rich as Lillie du Lac claims, I thought.

One thing about Wade Howell: she never flaunted the money angle. In fact, it was the one extreme of existence that she seemed to avoid.

"Not at all," I said, trying to sound bored. "I'm used to all kinds."

"Of course, with your mother keeping a boardinghouse."

A spasm of anger sent my mind scurrying to the dirty corners of the hall for consolation. All I could come up with was one of my mother's old maxims: "A sloppy housekeeper has sloppy morals." But that would never do. It distorted my impression of the pink plump matron in her tangle of useless appendages and false impressions. Since she was incapable of conjuring up the beauty required to keep love alive, it was only fitting that love should grope for more fertile ground to sink its roots. In our brief passage through the dark hall, I had lost all sympathy for Mrs. Howell. Once again, it pleased me to think that she was being deceived.

Slowly a triangle of sparkling light spread across the hall, and slowly I turned in the direction of its source. A young Mexican boy stood grinning by the open door. I followed Mrs. Howell toward the light, where I was allowed a brief but dazzling glimpse of the intricate web of the wealthy, which is at the same time transparent and stifling. The room was only a glittering display, a mausoleum to the living, but nonetheless I was momentarily impressed, which perhaps justified its existence. She led me quickly over dark polished floors, through white walls, red pillows, and gold candelabras, and down three marble steps onto a terrace where gold leaves grew in purple dust. Down below, half hidden by a Mexican sundial, a red-faced man in khaki shorts was furiously pulling weeds from a tangled bed of roses.

"I don't know what has come over the Colonel," she said. "He came in a little while ago fired with energy. Look at him sweat down there. And we're expecting guests for dinner.

"Howe," she screamed, "it's almost six."

He raised his hand impatiently, as though to silence her, and went back to his weeds.

"I don't know what has come over him," she repeated. "Now that I think of it, he's been acting funny ever since we came here." She hesitated. "Kind of restless, you know."

For an instant things seemed too much for her. Then she continued.

"I thought perhaps sending Dede away would help."

Sensing, or perhaps expecting, my astonishment, she hastily repaired her statement.

"Not that I would send her away for that reason. Dede comes first, of course."

With rapid little steps across the cobblestone, she ducked out from under the brief shadow of her husband to prove to me what I never doubted. I followed her up a delightful little back stairway washed in familiar pink. At the top was an enormous room that ran the entire width of the house. It was pink, of course. The walls were padded in a quilted pink material and squared off every three inches or so with a knot of yarn like a baby's blanket. We waded ankle-deep in pink fluff to get a better look at a round bed flounced in enough white tulle to come out at any cotillion. And if that wasn't enough, and apparently it wasn't, the ceiling was a mirror.

"Wade simply adores pink," Mrs. Howell said.

"I know. I saw the preview."

"That's very good," she commented without laughing. "I never was able to surprise anyone...not completely."

"Or perhaps not intentionally," I murmured under my breath.

I thought of the dull hall and the sparkling living room. The dark sources of a vast fortune that would surely be unearthed as pink bills. Even the Colonel's flabby flesh was tinged with its stifling rays. I thought of the girl who had made a desperate move to my airy room for a breath of freedom, only to find the windows jammed shut and the mocking face of the sun itself casting a strange new rose-tainted glow. God, what a stupidly powerful woman.

"Dede will be eighteen tomorrow, and this is her birthday surprise."

At least she succeeded in surprising me. It was less the eighteen that threw me off than its unfamiliar sound. I shared my room with Wade Howell, but I knew nothing about her. She had struck up a pose, and I had accepted it without question. I flipped back through my shallow acquaintances, and I shuddered to think that was the case all the way down the line. I was as hollow as this vacuous woman. Yet a moment before, in a rush of self-conscious judgment, I was about to pronounce her "the one most deserving of deception." Then, however briefly, she would be weighted down with the dubious crown while I, in our eternal round of comparison, would be buoyed on in my Dr Pepper float. Ah, but the moment was past and forgotten. Now I would have to fall back on my own little haven for the ego, "the one most deserving of understanding." Then, in a flash of hideous enlightenment, I wondered why. She, at least, loved her daughter. I loved no one. Least of all myself.

"Eighteen is a very important age for a girl...don't you think?"

"Yes, I guess it is."

"Of course, you wouldn't know. How old are you?"

"Twenty."

"Oh, I wouldn't have guessed it. You seem much younger."

Ordinarily this would make me angry. Now it made me gloomy. But the subtle nuances of mood were entirely lost on her. And this was her salvation. She would never know her daughter. But how quickly she always returned to the only subject that interested her.

"And then it will make a charming room for the young couple."

"Yes," I said, realizing that everything was a question to one who was constantly seeking reassurance.

"My room is just on the other side of the wall."

"Yes, indeed," I thought.

I took one last look at the double pink fluff and followed her down the stairs.

At the bottom, she turned to me and said, "Tomorrow morning I'm coming to take Dede home."

This, at least, did not surprise me.

◆　◆　◆

Downstairs everything was so glaringly normal that I felt I had lost the thread that would lead me back to a shady spot. In the living room, behind a bowl of fresh yellow roses, a showered powdered couple were sipping cocktails. The Colonel's lady, once again all a flutter with delight, introduced me to Major Morris and his mother, at the same time ignoring the Colonel, who was cracking ice behind a screen of flimsy silk dotted with red and gold butterflies.

But the Colonel, with an easy gesture of warm friendliness, called out, "I hope you're taking good care of our little girl."

You should know, I thought.

But all I said was, "I hope so too," and I felt stupid and dirty.

"It's not easy—is it?"

And his tone of intimate sincerity brought tears to my eyes. It was bad enough standing before these hygienically clean people without oozing emotion all over the place. I wished I could stay and prove myself, but the Colonel's lady had a tight grip on my shoulder and an impatient horn was tooting out front. But still I was reluctant to go, for as long as I stood rooted in wall-to-wall chenille, soaking up the fumes of Chanel No. 5, I had a vague yet familiar feeling of being up against something solidly substantial. It was the same sensation that I experienced when I thought about my grandmother who had seen me through school.

One thing was certain, it wasn't the uniform that drew me to the Colonel, for I had been pressed against enough hard-starched suntans lately to make the distinction. And I had never allowed myself to regard well-ordered triviality with anything but disdain. Well, he obviously possessed dignity and kindliness, but was that reason enough for the women to topple all over him?

"Eunice is making a big thing of Wade's birthday—kind of 'goodbye girlhood, hello womanhood' sort of thing," he laughed. "And this young lady was kind enough to keep her diverted for a week." The Colonel was explaining me to his friends.

At the same time, I felt him studying me through the screen.

"And a good job she's done, too."

Although his tone was pompous, I sensed that this gauzy glance was anything but. If only he'd come out from behind that screen, I felt certain he would tuck a yellow rosebud in my buttonhole as he gave me a thorough going-over. Then his eyes would meet mine in lavish appreciation for what he saw. At that moment I would have done anything for the Colonel. But the little rosebud meant goodbye. I submitted to Mrs. Howell's urgent tug.

"The experience has done her no harm. In fact, it might have done her a world of good. Sometimes I think Eunice keeps her too close. But then, she isn't my daughter."

No indeed. But none the less a susceptible subject for a dignified shoulder and a kindly hand.

"Well, she'll soon be all yours—eh, Major?"

At the door, I turned and was startled to find that Major Morris, who had appeared a stranger up close, looked familiar from a distance. He had gotten up to examine the glittering collection of cut crystal jewel cases that rested in comfortable splendor in a little gilt cabinet lined with white tufted satin. The Colonel's lady apparently believed that the most prized possessions were those requiring tender tedious care. I thought of the Colonel's air of forthright solidarity that oozed out from all his fragile disguises. I suspected that his second wife had acquired him at great expense and much trouble to use as a tufted backdrop for someone she considered more important.

Major Morris was apparently feeling his drinks, for the sparkling treasures rattled in his hand. On the other side of the yellow roses, Mrs. Morris, snug in her belief that her son was marrying well, contentedly blew smoke rings, which at one point formed a gray cloud that created exactly the illusion of half-darkness I was groping for. I realized that Major Morris was the tall dark man who had greeted Wade Howell at the door of the little bungalow. As I observed his deliberate movements and indecisive attitude, he no longer reminded me of Gerald Eaton. Yet I could not be certain whether he was the man who had called on Wade the first night she had stayed at the Angus. That, I thought, was my hope.

Back in the hall I was surprised at the neat manner in which Mrs. Howell packaged up my visit, verbally putting me in her debt.

"I know you've enjoyed seeing Dede's home. Now don't give away my little surprise, but I do want her to be pleased. Wouldn't you be pleased?"

I knew that she hadn't called me out for an inspection tour, so I immediately latched onto the clue: she wanted me to smooth the way for tomorrow—to make certain it wouldn't be a disappointment. In the end, all that really counted in her world was the appearance.

This didn't strike me as unusual. Around every casual corner, one is confronted with bits of tightly tangled lives and asked for a donation of approval to support the mess. A nod, a smile, even an attentive expression will do. But it is simple enough, for it is understood by all that the gesture is purely mechanical. So, of course, I was ready with my little nod, and Mrs. Howell accepted it for what it was worth.

All the time, I was looking at a dreary cathedral-style mirror over the chair where the Colonel's blouse had hung. In the dust on the mirror was printed "shit." Mrs. Howell saw it too, for she edged over to the other side of the hall and stood with her back to the dirty word.

I noticed that she was really quite plump, and it was only her slender shapely legs that saved her from appearing fat.

"Like Colette's cashiers," I thought.

This thought amused me, while I thanked my hostess for a wonderful afternoon. Then I hurried down the stairs to the limousine. Only after I was settled behind the PFC did I realize that no one had thought to offer me any refreshments. This was unheard of in my mother's house.

◆　◆　◆

Back at the Angus, I found my room empty. I turned the sheet, pulled the curtains open, and fell on my face into a heavy sleep. I dreamed of an ugly house full of footlockers where soldiers, dressed in tufted khaki, marched aimlessly up and down stairs and through endless halls.

When I woke up, it was dark. It took me a long while to return in time and place. I heard the hillbilly band from the Saddle Club down the street. They were playing "San Fernando Valley." This had been a very long day, and now it was Saturday night. I itched all over.

I took a long cool shower and dressed carefully in a red linen skirt and a white piqué blouse. For some inexplicable reason, I felt wonderful.

"I get this airy feeling at the damnedest times," I thought, as I brushed on some greasy bright red lipstick.

But not having a date seemed rather a luxury. I looked forward to an evening at the Angus, for even on dull nights there was a feeling of unexpected fun lurking in the shadows.

When I left my room, an untimely light pulled me toward

Lillie du Lac's door. Ordinarily my mother and her friend would be topping off a late dinner with some of Lillie's piping hot black coffee.

"As usual, he had his own explanation, which he gave quietly, gently, and without batting an eye, the old smoothie—and I don't believe a word of it." Lillie had apparently recovered sufficiently from her burst of anger to regain her coherence.

I had no intention of standing there eavesdropping. As it was, I was thoroughly disgusted with myself. If I had any character at all, I would have simply gone up to Wade and told her to leave. Instead, I had sat by and allowed her to burst in on my privacy and to carry on to such a degree that I was not certain that what I saw was really so, or instead the results of my exhaustion and need to be alone. And I had to be alone. Otherwise I forgot who I was. I lost all sense of judgment. Who said that all we have left in the modern world are a few little secrets? Oscar Wilde, perhaps. A shiver of fear came over me when I thought of my foolish picnic with Richard Randolph Atlas III. There simply had to be some empty hours to pry the hideously mangled parts from the smoldering rubbish heap.

Well, tomorrow I would be alone. But through no fault of my own. As usual, I had simply stood by, weak-willed and whimpering, and allowed time and chance to pull me through. This was merely a moment's black realization. On the whole, I felt wonderful—clean and rested and reasonable.

"Come in!" Lillie du Lac's voice was in a gay key that seemed only a trifle flat.

When she looked at me, I thought I detected just a little of the ewe, but there was still enough of the ram to keep her from going completely woolly. At any rate, it was better than her former attitude of insulting antagonism. She was mending the dust ruffle, while my mother dabbed gold paint on the frame of the mirror that had already been replaced. They must have skipped dinner to patch up the damage.

Lillie motioned me to a little wire chair in the corner. The tip of a concave heart dug into my back at a sensitive spot. I sat up, straight and uncomfortable, while they continued a conversation that had started in January.

"It's your own fault," my mother said. "You weren't satisfied with seeing him—you had to let everyone know about it."

"I didn't bring the girl here."

"No, but you were considering it. I remember that Sunday when the picture came out—how you all banged your heads together with plots and schemes."

"But the fact remains that it was her mother's idea, or her idea, and now I'm beginning to think he had something to do with it."

"He admitted Wade took him by surprise at the top of the stairs. What more do you want?"

"That's so like him. He never could bear unpleasantness, so he lies." Lillie stood up, tall and bony and angry. "But there she was half-naked—the front half—when I opened my door to let him in."

Ah, so Lillie had been expecting him! Her eye was too clever not to realize the potential chic of the Turkish towel.

"She seems like such a lady, too."

"Martha, will you stop thinking like a servant and let the dead past you know what."

"You're a good one to be talking about digging up the dead."

"The Colonel came here on his own—he was thirsty for a decent cup of coffee. I didn't call him. I didn't even write him a polite little note on his promotion."

Lillie sat down on the window seat and christened the new mirror with a gay little smile.

"Come to think of it, I didn't congratulate him on any of his promotions. He got his second lieutenant's bar on the day the divorce went through."

She made a neat little spiral with her right index finger.

"And, of course, I remained heartbroken for a decent interval."

Now she paused for a decent interval to allow the drama of the past to overtake the present.

"First lieutenant, captain, major . . . they all came so fast that I hardly had time to wipe my eyes."

Lillie's lips kept moving, but all we heard was Frank Sinatra singing "Paper Doll." And the nickel played out.

"Then one day an overheated colonel came puffing into the courtyard to get out of the sun . . ."

All at once, from my place in the corner, I made the announcement.

"I went out to the Howells's this afternoon," I said in a low flat voice, deliberately minimizing the impression it had made on me.

Lillie refused to be impressed.

"The layaway plan has broken down more social barriers than the French Revolution," she said.

But even Lillie du Lac wasn't a flawless performer.

All at once I was the center of attention. I could have sworn that the rooster stretched his neck and turned his head in my direction.

"And what was the second Mrs. Howell doing?"

"Nothing much...except that she's finished decorating Wade's room. It's all in—"

"Don't tell me, now." Lillie made a mock expression of grave perplexity. "It's pink," she said triumphantly.

"How did you know?"

"I keep an open mind—and an open door."

"What did she have to say?" This, of course, was my mother.

"Martha, please. Just when I was enjoying myself, you have to turn on the lights."

"She's coming to get Wade tomorrow."

"No! Not really? But then, she hasn't seen what a perfect charmer she's become in the last week. She's warm and friendly— why, she's completely come out." Lillie turned to me, all twists and angles. "You saw her this afternoon. Did she look ready for ruffles and flounces and pink party bows?"

And Lillie du Lac was lost in bitter thought. As for me, I was thinking about my back. I couldn't stand that sharp little chair much longer. When I got up, the rooster crowed and Lillie threw the scissors at it. The handle caught on the cage, the point hanging down and swinging back and forth in a torturous-looking movement. I saw that she regretted this insane violence.

Since I got us into this tricky subject, I thought, it's up to me to set the keynote, a slightly weary joy.

"I thought you'd be glad to see her go," I said.

God, what an afternoon with a strong-willed woman could do. I was talking like her. Doing everyone's little thinking.

"There's always a little regret in everything...even in getting your own way." She smiled and looked rather mild—at least for Lillie.

"To tell you the truth, if she hadn't gone soon, I would have burned down the place."

At the door, I turned and said, "Colonel Howell is charming."

"I'm beginning to have hope for you." Then, to my mother: "With Sergeant McCane gone and the Colonel gone, we'll have to start living for the young."

And we all laughed until we cried.

◆   ◆   ◆

From the balcony at the end of the hall, I looked down on the courtyard and saw two girls dangling on the wall. Piece by piece, I put them together: dungarees, T-shirts, earrings, bracelets, and long dirty bobs. In short, tavern girls of the Southwest. From up above, they had appeared to be identical twins, but now that we were all on the same level, I noticed that one was plain without the genetic paradox of one gross feature, while the other was distinctive in having the flattest face I had ever seen.

Later I learned from Jess that this disfigurement was the result of a bizarre accident. "No Nose," as she came to be known, was caught sideways in the safety door of a rapid transit bus. Right where "Please wait for the green light, then push the door" met "Por favor espere la luz verde." Her nose was flattened to the point of seeming concave. Fortunately, for No Nose at least, suing the transit company in San Antonio had reached the stage where it was almost a municipal lottery. This, of course, was part of our Mexican heritage, and was slyly winked upon as local color. A crack in the sidewalk or a hole in the street was worth a half hour's attention any time, for one could depend on any number of Mexicans risking their necks for a chance in the game.

No Nose, as the story goes, got a fabulous amount of money for damages. And from that time on, she had wandered about in a kind of half-trance, spending all of her time and most of her money in the bars up and down South Alamo.

But of course when I got to the bottom of the stairs, I was not acquainted with the tragic facts of No Nose's accident. I felt clean and haughty in the presence of Jess and his two visitors. I wrapped myself in a shallow pose of stuffiness and regretted my Saturday night.

All at once, Jess put down *Crime and Punishment* and sat up on his ragged cot. Why in the world did he have to create such a realistic setting for his reading?

"What we need around here is more passion," he said.

The two girls began to giggle, and Jess looked at them as though he had forgotten they were there.

"Duchess, I want you to meet Burma and No Nose. Dolls, ain't they? Alamo dollies, you might call them."

"He's crazy." This was the one called Burma, who despite the name—which I suspected she had lifted from *Terry and the Pirates*—and the absence of any disgusting disfigurement was the more ghastly of the two. No Nose was clearly the leader, and considering the foggy expression and irresolute movements of Burma, she was performing a greater service than she realized.

"Where's Wade?" Jess said, and I shuddered.

For the moment, I was stung by the purely fanciful notion that his sudden mention of Wade Howell was brought about by these two girls. Their weak dependence upon each other reminded him of my relation to Wade. At first this thought disturbed me more than the fact that he might be thinking about her from his own point of view. Of course, I was certain that he had no consuming interest in those freaks on the wall, and he probably hadn't thought about them in any connection. On the other hand, no man, as far as I knew, had ever dismissed Wade Howell lightly. I didn't think that he cared for her any more than perhaps Mira, but she must have intrigued him. I felt guilty. He'd had a bad time, and I didn't wish to hurt him anymore. It had been thoughtless of me to bring Wade to the Angus in the first place. But there again was my weak will.

There was a wild jangle of bracelets as the two girls jumped off the wall.

"What did I tell you?" Jess said, with mock seriousness. "Even if that painter does show up, you two couldn't sit still for five minutes without itchin' and scratchin' around."

Apparently another amateur artist had made a wild promise while painting in the courtyard of the Angus.

"You don't think we're pretty enough to paint—that's what."

Fortunately, just then Lillie du Lac came down the stairs. Her expression became quizzically amused as she glanced from Jess to the two girls.

"Martha, if you can see your way to facing the public . . . ," she called back up the stairs to my mother, who had stopped off on the balcony to spray for roaches.

Then she adjusted her southern belle manner for the benefit of No Nose and Burma. "I haven't had a breath of air all day. My skin is so fair it was never meant for the heat of day."

"It's that dry head of hair you'd better watch," my mother called over the railing. "If the sun ever gets a chance at those chemicals, you'll go up in flame."

Then she spied the two girls, and she came running down the stairs.

"I told you two not to come around here. You give the Angus a bad name."

"An artist is going to make a painting of us—right here. *Study in Decadence*, he's going to call it," No Nose said proudly.

"Your portraits won't be painted in my courtyard. Indeed! Do you realize the Angus is practically a public shrine?"

"So are they, Maw. So are they."

Suddenly, Burma, in a fit of aggression, came closer to my mother.

"Honey, I love your hairdo," she said to Jess.

Then, spotting some little sandwiches that had been left on the table, she was temporarily distracted. She went through a picky polite business of trying to decide which one to choose.

"Don't eat those," Lillie du Lac said. "They've been in the hot sun all day."

Jess grinned and said, "They can't hurt her."

I was amused to think that earlier I had a similar thought about Wade Howell. There was an element of truth in Jess's flippant remark. It sometimes seems that in the very act of destruction, one builds up a certain strength, a kind of immunity to the world of reality. This was nothing more than a thought of the moment, and later I was to realize how fragile it was.

No Nose, too, had latched onto Jess's remark and was amused in her fashion. She moved close to him on the cot and said, "Honey, you're all there."

"Honey, what happened to you?" Jess said.

"It's a long story."

"And I've got plenty of time."

"Who did you say did your hair?" No Nose said, in a clumsy attempt to change the subject.

But Burma was jealous. "I noticed it first," she complained. "I wish you would leave me something."

"Come on, Honey," Jess said to No Nose. "Let's you and me reminisce."

It was at this point that Jess, his blond hair and tan face a perfect background for the devilish expression that played such a fascinating game with his features that one was never quite certain how he really looked, learned how No Nose's face became her fortune. And the rest of us were diverted from this tête-à-tête when the soft velvet cloak of southern gentility once again slipped from Lillie's shoulders.

"Why, you old horse's ass," she said, looking up to the balcony. "A person can't turn around without running into a shitty relative."

At various times Gibson had been a cowboy, a horse trainer, a gambler, a rancher, and a sheriff. He was wise and tough and Texan. He was afraid of nothing—except Lillie du Lac in public. When he spotted her on the street, he always ducked into the nearest bar to avoid the spray of words that was certain to shrink him down to size. He hadn't come to the Angus for nothing.

Her slant-eyed, high-headed appearance, the constant note of mocking disapproval in her voice, and the gracefully disdainful movements of her body commanded a degree of respect. Gibson, being no fool, recognized these qualities for what they were— the defenses of dignity necessary to keep a loving sensitive soul intact.

He did not answer her in her own tone. Instead, he took off his ten-gallon hat, bowed his head slightly, and said, "Ma'am, I don't like to trouble you...bring you any bad news ..."

"Nonsense," Lillie du Lac said, "you're delighted. Otherwise you wouldn't be so quick with the manners."

It surprised me that Lillie sounded so genuinely irritated. I would have thought that Gibson's hard masculinity would have appealed to her.

"I'm sworn to certain duties," Gibson went on.

"Cripes!" Lillie said. "Stop talking and start swearing."

A little fat pig-face poked out from behind the bony shoulders of the sheriff. The face was red and swollen with tears. Gibson stepped aside and there was Mira, as unironed and unkempt as she had been the first morning she came dragging into the courtyard after Jess.

It had been several days since we had seen her. To be precise, the day after she had tagged after the photographers in quest of a whiff of fame. Lillie du Lac and I had been alone when Mira had bounced into the courtyard in her little pig uniform.

"Guess what?" she had said, without warning or greeting.

"We despise guessing games," Lillie said coldly, while I kept one eye on *The Skin of Our Teeth* and the other on the happy little pig.

"I got a job at the Little Pig Stand selling pork barbecue. Tommy's locked up safe now and the cadet's out of danger. I'm walking on clouds."

"Do you think you can handle it?" Lillie said.

"There's not much to it. I go in tomorrow for my training course."

"I've been there," I said. "Instead of handing out a menu, the waitresses come up and say *oink oink*. It's gruesome."

"No, like this," and Mira let out a squeal that sounded like a real pig.

"They do a remarkable job of placing people these days," was all Lillie said.

Then she went into her kitchen, I went back to my book, and Mira drifted away from the courtyard.

Now the sheriff was saying, "This lil' ol' gal has herself some trouble."

Jess got up from the cot and stood in the middle of the court-yard looking up at Mira. The two dollies, who had suddenly jelled into a solid mass at the sight of the sheriff, looked about to spill out all over the wall at any moment. But there wasn't so much as a tinkle of a charm from their bracelets. We were all facing in one direction like animals against the wind. We were waiting for the sheriff to continue.

"A heap of trouble, if you want the truth of the matter."

"By all means."

"She was selling beer…after hours," Gibson proclaimed harshly to the soft night, at the same time feigning sensitivity to the expectant faces below. "And what's more, she's under age."

At this point, the sheriff became absolutely stunned with the burden of his office. After all, what other stand could an honor-able man take in the face of all that under and over with nothing just right? He seemed to shrink. Or perhaps it was because Mira, who was a big girl, had stepped out ahead of him. Her eyes were hollow and her usually full face was pinched to the point where she seemed to be inhaling a nasty odor. I thought of the rosy girl who had left in a flash of glory less than a week before. Time can't approach intensity of emotion when it comes to bringing about change.

"And what's more, it turns out she's not even married."

Mira burst into tears, as though on cue. Later, much later, we laughed about it, saying it was like a typical San Antone shower, coming as it did without warning. Always alert to the slightest shift in mood, Lillie du Lac skimmed to the top of the stairs, took Mira in her arms, and backed the sheriff to the wall with one of her high-cheeked she-devil looks. He muttered something about "Someone has to be responsible" and instantly dropped out of sight into the dark hall.

"Responsible indeed," Lillie shouted from the balcony. "I'll take the place of ten policemen."

Jess was waiting at the bottom of the stairs to help Mira to the cot. My mother brought a boric acid wash and clean rags from the kitchen. And the little pig sobbed out her sad story while Lillie changed the wet wads on her eyes and Jess held her hand.

It seemed that Tommy Faraday already had one wife when he married Mira. Thus, in a few turbulent days, she had found that her marriage was illegal, her child was illegitimate, and her life was insignificant. Jess was all tenderness.

"I hope you've learned that simply latching onto a man doesn't make the difference," was Lillie's only comment.

I sensed that she shared my aversion to this sodden mood. After all, the atmosphere had been pushing down rather heavy all day, and it was high time for a relief. But in order not to appear insensitive, it was necessary to go about it gradually.

"You don't like Gibson, do you?" I said to Lillie. I had certainly taken to the language of the acquisitive.

"Anything that is in excess is in bad taste." Her tone was mild

until she came to the last few words. "Gibson is too much man."
With this, her voice scratched and her face became a bony triangle of sharp angles. I felt certain she was thinking of her evoca-
tive ex-husband. What was that gentle charm he possessed? Of
course, it was nothing more than a wisp of effeminacy.

The two girls on the wall took this as a sudden relaxation of
discipline. In this new mellowed atmosphere, they began scratching around and giggling. Suddenly Lillie du Lac hurled the bowl
of boric acid solution in the direction of the disturbance. The
Alamo dollies slipped off the wall and went screaming into the
night like two stray cats.

"It's girls like that give women a bad name," Jess said.

As for me, they gave me a kind of security. While they were
there, I felt like a combination Rita Hayworth and Madame
Chiang. As Lillie du Lac always said, "One always gets a lift in
the company of inferiors."

◆ ◆ ◆

The day had been a chore all around. I realized this in the tired
lines of my mother's face and the powdery whiteness of her
skin. Her sagging appearance, however, was due less to strained
emotions than to overwork. The first thing in the morning, she
had decided that Francisco, the maid, was too pregnant to work.
She stuffed two ten-dollar bills into the young Mexican's apron
pocket and told her to come back when she felt better.

"Mrs. Saunders, I will work for you until you die," Francisco
had said. And she meant it.

In the meantime, there were floors to mop, beds to make, and dirty basins to polish. Then there was the constant nuisance of transients to settle in clean fresh rooms. My mother had worked hard through the long hot hours. By the time she had made her way to the aggravating incident with the old soldier, she was in no mood to be crossed. After that, there must have followed the strenuous ordeal with Lillie, which was hardly a substitute for a relaxing dinner. Now, at seven, she was faced with a courtyard full of tension. What she needed was a shot on the rocks; what came was a blast of another kind.

Sergeant McCane, his homely wife, and little retarded daughter piled out of the taxi. They had been traveling from Memphis on a slow crowded train. All day and half the night they had shuffled about with suitcases and shopping bags. They were hot and tired and dirty. The little girl kept babbling incoherently.

When my mother was tired, her actions were unpredictable. She had no patience with these weary travelers.

"Surely you didn't expect me to hold your room indefinitely?"

Sergeant McCane did. "I would have paid you," he said.

"I'm not a mind reader."

"Steady there, Maw," Jess said.

But she was in no mood to be appeased. She turned away when Sergeant McCane introduced his wife and child. He had probably boasted to his wife that the Angus was like a second home, and now that little conceit had been snatched away. There was nothing for him to do but start looking for a room on Saturday night when a cot in the hall went for a dollar.

It had always seemed to me that my mother chose to evict her roomers during intervals charged with meaning. In the midst of a sentimental interlude or an ironic turn of events. This made the evictions seem more frequent than they really were. They brought to mind a chorus. A mocking refrain of our crazy existence at the Angus during those summer months of the war.

Now Wade Howell, in full mourning, followed by Gerry Eaton and Swarthout, was coming toward the courtyard. The music of the poor began ringing in my ears. We had money enough at that time. I guess everyone did. But we never lost the habit of feeling poor.

Jess and I arranged the family's luggage in the taxi while my mother glared at us. The little girl was crying. Sergeant McCane closed the door of the taxi as though he were sealing himself into a tomb.

"He must have had his eyes closed when he married her," I heard Gerry Eaton say. And the pains of anger in my throat brought tears to my eyes.

The anger was directed at my own cheap trivial emotions. Gerry Eaton was merely a symbol to remind me again of the hideous mediocrity that crept in from all sides. It was small. It was nagging. But it was cruel. Above all, it was synthetic. If we had been honest, we could not have failed to recognize our feelings for what they were: tawdry ornaments to disguise our makeshift garment. In the end, perhaps, the decoration would weigh us down. We would come apart at the seams and all stand shivering in the sun.

"Hello, Mrs. Saunders," Wade said.

"Real colorful." This was Swarthout, who was spinning around dizzily in the confusion of the courtyard.

For a moment I wanted to rush up to all of them and explain that my mother wasn't really like that, and the only time she resorted to shoddiness was when she was tired, but the taxi drove away, the moment passed, and I no longer cared. I knew what she was really like.

"It smells like a man in there," she mumbled. "The whole room will have to be gone over with essence of pine." With this, she pushed past my friends and went upstairs.

There was no use interfering. Nothing would restore her but a long night's rest. By Monday she would be tracking down her roomers through an intricate chain of calls to all the little hotels in the city.

◆　◆　◆

It was plain to see that our gathering behind the Angus was doomed from the beginning. The exact set of circumstances and the precise mood had not come together to bring harmony to a diversified group of people. In short, there was an illusion of such frightening normality that no one dared to be himself. The two cadets were polite and uncomfortable. Jess, instead of being amiably funny, was listless and disinterested. He merely wiggled his artificial foot in acknowledgment of the introduction. Mira sat on the wall with her back to us and looked out upon the city. Wade was more restless than usual, constantly tapping her foot as though to lure us off on a hectic chase through the back streets. And I was stupefied with confusion.

Later, as we left the Angus, I experienced a tugging little half-realization that I was annoyed by this "surprise" call. Apparently Wade had arranged the whole thing as a kind of combination truce and birthday celebration. But I detested parties almost as much as I did roommates. Both are presumptuous breaches of privacy.

Lillie du Lac, of course, showed signs of life.

"You're fliers?" She had learned more from her wealthy former employers than how to make excellent coffee.

"The army isn't under that impression," Cadet Eaton snapped.

"Now isn't that grand? There's a great future there—trips to the moon and all."

And I, in turn, had learned a great deal from Lillie du Lac.

"Gerry's looking for a place that doesn't have a president," I said.

Gerry, who took himself seriously, glared at me, but Jess smiled in appreciation. Then he offered his usual final words.

"Sometimes I think, well...and then again, I just don't know."

He rolled over and went to sleep. There would be no party at the Angus that night.

◆   ◆   ◆

I was right about the little get-together being a peace offering from Wade. The four of us were no sooner arranged in a plush half-moon on the dark side of the Tropics when she slipped a tiny envelope into my hand.

"Don't open it until you're alone," she whispered.

I smiled vaguely, stuffed the envelope into my bag, and promptly lost interest in it. Wade Howell's ridiculous little acts of petty intrigue were becoming intolerable. Besides, Gerry Eaton was very close to me.

"I would rather be here than any place in the whole world," I said, to make up for the nasty remark back in the courtyard.

"You're perfect," he said. "You never spoil a party."

I shivered as he mixed the precious Canadian Club with Coca-Cola.

"Mediocrity and all it connotes is the most tasteless thing under the sun," I thought, but I kept quiet.

When Gerry called for a toast, all I could think of was "God save us from the great middle class," so I kept quiet. Nor did I allow myself to be tempted by "To a long and happy marriage." Apparently I was trying to live up to my small reputation as the perfect date. That, at least, excused my timidity for the evening.

In the end, we drank to "Happy birthday, dear Wade." Then we danced to "Imagine you imagining that you love me." After that, Gerry requested "Sleepy Time Down South," and we kissed while the band fumbled around among the pages of sheet music. We utilized every minute in those days. Besides, this had become our "theme song." That was all right, because Gerry's wife lived in Milwaukee or Minneapolis, I never knew which, and it would have held little meaning for her.

I had decided not to mention the fact that I knew Gerry was married. After all, it would serve no purpose except to show that he wasn't putting anything over on me. And what was that beside the risk of spoiling our holiday mood and the wispy memory we would no doubt cherish forever?

"You're wonderful," Gerry said.

I didn't argue with him. His remark served to punctuate my point: the less we said and the more we danced and smooched, the sweeter the memory.

"You may think that I object to your being so Bohemian and all . . ."

But I couldn't prevent him from talking. And the more he talked, the less I thought of him. Bohemian, indeed! To me the word meant freedom. The sweet freedom of the noble. The true nobility. The nobility of purpose, character, and accomplishment.

"What I mean is your background."

I let him fall overboard without so much as tossing him a life ring.

"It doesn't make me think any less of you."

Perhaps not, but I thought less of him with every syllable.

"In fact, it makes you more interesting."

You'll never be anything but a ward heeler, I thought.

Swarthout was motioning us back to the table. At first I thought that Wade Howell had some urgent whim. But then I saw that she was entangled in an enormous T-bone, and from her diabolical expression, I expected her to devour it bones and all. After that, perhaps some careless scraps, the one luxury of the poor, from Swarthout's untidy plate.

Wade Howell would be content for hours. It was Swarthout who found the place dead. We would have to move on.

"There must be some place in this burg with signs of life," he grumbled.

This attitude of boredom toward our city by the soldiers and their wives irritated me to the point of scratching anger.

"Someday you'll realize that you never had it so good," I predicted.

But when I became older, I realized that most people are completely lacking in sensitivity to and harmony with the world in which they live. In a larger sense, that is. Unless they are surrounded by their own familiar possessions and a few habitual friends, all is meaningless. There is nothing under the sun to interest them.

We packed up the Canadian Club and took a taxi to a long, low rambling place called the Tower. It was enormous. Room after shadowy room. And the possibility for amusement seemed infinite against the cheap glow of pink and green and blue lights. Everyone came here. As we waited in line for a table, it struck me that perhaps there was some significance in the name. This was our Mecca.

"A cheap trick," I heard someone say, "no matter how you look at it."

Even so there was something about the place, for I began to like Gerry again. In a half hour we were seated on a windy terrace, where we had to anchor our paper cups with ice cubes while Gerry mixed the drinks.

"One thing about this place," I said, "it's so dark you can't tell the waitresses from the debutantes."

No one was amused except Wade Howell, of all people, who had no sense of humor to speak of. For all our pains, Swarthout still looked glum.

"He got his divorce," Gerry explained, as we watched Wade and Swarthout slip behind a palm tree.

"That's what he wanted," I said through what I intended as a sophisticated puff of smoke.

"He's not sure now—she was the most beautiful redhead."

"They always are, to hear you men talk. But it's all the same. He can still cry in his beer over the beautiful redhead."

I was being deliberately malicious.

"Say, what's gotten into you?"

"Nothing yet, and I intend to keep it that way."

I looked into a pair of gray eyes that were more hurt than shocked, and I realized I had spoken out loud. Our carefully casual yet deeply respectful relationship had been shriveled into the unregenerate commonplace by a few poisonous words.

"It's too late now," was all he said for what seemed like five minutes.

"I knew I should have told you I was married. I knew it when we were dancing in the sawdust of the International Club. I knew it on our long taxi rides to the field. I knew it an hour ago at the Tropics... but time was always getting short, and I thought it would blow over, and we'd have had our little time together. Now it's too late."

I loved Gerry Eaton at that moment as I sat and cried.

It's too late... too late... too late, kept ringing in my ears.

Ten minutes before, I had been the smooth sophisticate.

"I didn't tell you I loved you, either," Gerry said earnestly. "I guess I figured that one forbearance might cancel out the other...the hair shirt idea, you know."

I knew indeed. Although I saw Gerry's declaration for the sodden little mess it was, I was rather proud to have been his object of love at that time—our time. That was something his wife didn't have, or even Wade Howell, for that matter. And to think that I had put an end to it with my own words! I was elated. Here was a keepsake I could take back to my room with pride.

"All I ask is if we ever meet again, you will say, 'Hi, there goes the girl I had fun with.'"

Gerry put his arm around me and said, "What I like is a girl who can be promiscuous as hell on Saturday night and sing in the choir on Sunday morning."

"Or can swim in the nude without asking what you think of her morals."

He gave me a knowing little squeeze. We had pigeonholed our brief love, and now all that remained was to play it out with grace. That proved harder than I anticipated.

Swarthout and Wade Howell went around the tree on their way back to the table. I swallowed my tears and slipped behind a mask of cynical understanding. I was convinced that nothing more was to come of this relationship with Gerry Eaton, and I was satisfied that I had played out my part rather well.

"Anyway, Swarthout has his war to fight," I said.

"It won't last forever."

"I never thought of that," I said regretfully.

"No one does. Least of all the army."

The music stopped. Gerry ordered champagne cocktails and hors d'oeuvres. The cocktails were brought immediately, but we would have to wait for the hors d'oeuvres. I expected that. The Mexicans, no doubt, were sent scurrying all over town for hot peppers, salami, and anchovy olives.

"Hail and farewell!" Gerry said, lifting his glass, and I knew this meant goodbye.

Swarthout and Wade fell right in with our sweet sad mood. Swarthout because he had lost his redhead and Wade for any one of a vast collection of elusive pretenses that seemed to spring forth at gatherings such as ours. The bigger the group, the more pronounced was her melancholy.

Gerry went on toasting in first one direction and then another, often referring to "our little group" and "the wonderful times we've had together." I couldn't help but feel that he would suddenly set down his glass, shake hands, and remind us to vote for him.

But it remained for me to be the guest of honor, for the rest of them had known all along that this was our last time together. Then, too, I sensed that this was a special time and place, and never again would it be quite the same. I couldn't expect them to share my feelings at that moment. After all, they knew beforehand what the evening implied.

Wade Howell insisted on dragging me off to the ladies' lounge, which I considered a frivolous waste of time.

"What did you tell mother about me?"

She splashed her face in icy water while three girls formed a line behind her.

"Nothing," I whispered, trying to conjure up a little intimacy in this screeching giggling room.

But Wade would have none of that.

"Nothing?" she shouted through five paper towels.

"No. Why should I tell her anything about you?"

"Then why did you go out there? I know you went. I heard you on the phone."

"She invited me, and I went. That's all there was to it."

"And you didn't talk about me?"

"I didn't say that."

"You did too."

"I said I didn't tell her about you. There's a difference."

I enjoyed her initial shiver of anger before I continued with my slow torment.

"She did the talking, as you can imagine ... and all it amounted to is that you're going home tomorrow."

And I tossed aside the tedious preparations of a week.

"I know that much."

There we were, two nasty little girls spitting words at each other while our playmates stood by and watched. Slowly Wade came closer to me, and for a moment, I thought she intended to claw me to pieces.

Instead she whispered, "You know very well that I wanted you to tell her all about me. Why do you think I act like that? And stay in your old room, for that matter?"

I was sick with anger and suppressed tears.

"I had no intention of telling your mother how you parade around naked all over the place in the hope that some man will notice you." I said this loud enough so that a hard little blond dropped her lipstick right in the middle of making a Bette Davis mouth.

"It wouldn't surprise me if there were bedbugs in your room."

This was her final slap before she sailed out through two doors. I went up in flames.

But outside Glenn Miller was blowing moondust all over the place, and Gerry Eaton was standing under a palm tree waiting to take me in his arms.

"You're wasting our precious time."

I began piling up memories like crazy at this point. Everything that happened in the dark blue palace seemed significant.

"What's the story on that girlfriend of yours?"

We hadn't said anything for minutes. Now the subject under discussion didn't please me at all.

"She doesn't get along with her mother—that's all."

But this didn't satisfy Gerry.

"She's engaged, isn't she?"

"Yes."

"Then what's she doing chasing around?"

I could have been nasty and reminded him that he too was chasing around, but I didn't want to spoil what little time we had left.

"She's having a fling before settling down."

"Sort of an extended bachelor dinner?"

"Yes. That's cute."

"Her idea of a fling and Swarthout's are entirely different. She's a pretty cold fish."

I smiled coolly, anticipating a rearrangement of this casual observation. A few words would do it. Perhaps a flippant description of my little room blazing with light through the hot night would be good for a laugh, and go on from there. I hesitated. A smoldering desire to get even with Wade was tinged with a loyalty of sorts.

For once I believed her. Perhaps that was it: I no longer questioned her. It seemed so normal that she should deliberately set out to cultivate a reputation for being "fast."

And not for herself, certainly. That was the clincher. It was a sacrifice, a protest against what went for normality. I thought of the lush pink woman with her ear to the wall and I shuddered.

But this was only a blurred, underdeveloped flash of the moment. I was not ready to act on it, for I was still untangling myself from that silly little self-imposed maze that had finally gotten snarled beyond repair.

"She may be cold to Swarthout, but she's playing it fast and loose with everyone else."

With these words, I wrote the end of our romance. Gerry stopped dancing and was staring at me. I couldn't decide whether he was disgusted or fascinated.

"Do you like Wade? Do you find her attractive?"

Then I regretted having brought up the subject. It stamped me as an envious cat.

"She's a queen, but I didn't figure I had time for her complex games."

I was prepared to surrender Gerry Eaton to his wife, but I couldn't bear to have him so much as think about Wade Howell, nor for her to think about him. The sooner we got back to our intimate across-the-table mood, the better. But first I had to keep Gerry from sinking deeper into the reverie that simply wouldn't release its hold in him. After all, this was my night. I had every right to his undivided attention.

Then, suddenly, he seemed to brush aside the thoughts without any help from me.

"There's no need to tell Swarthout about this—she suits his purpose for now. He's playing war, and she's a beautiful girl to decorate his khaki shoulder."

I had to admit that I couldn't have put it better myself. I was satisfied. He simply didn't want his buddy to get involved in another affair so soon after an unhappy marriage.

We danced to a distant dark corner of the terrace where behind a hedge of artificial boxwood, Gerry pressed me against a rough wall. A thousand sharp edges stuck into my back as he kissed my breath away. Then that pain was obliterated by another, deeper hurt. As I turned my head to the ancient weather-beaten wall, all I could think of was a primitive Spanish knife jabbing me again and again. Pleasure and pain became so confused that I imagined I was living my whole life in this meager paradise.

Only when we were dancing back to the table did I feel the dampness of my dress. The pain was less intense, but it was still there.

"There's something on your dress." This was Swarthout. But I was too disappointed at the realization that my pain was purely physical to be concerned about the bloody mess on the back of my dress, or that Wade Howell and Gerry Eaton had moved so close that her dark eyes cast shadows on his pale face.

Oddly enough, it was the self-pitying Swarthout who slipped a clean handkerchief into my hand and told me to have the attendant in the ladies' room fix me up. His big hand hid the spot on my dress as he led me to the door. For the first time, I thought about how good-looking he was with his blond hair and smooth rosy complexion. Until then, Swarthout had scarcely noticed me. And I had heard so much about his glorious redhead that I was certain he found me plain. I had comforted myself with the thought that it took a more thoughtful person than this to detect my subtle beauty.

"They should keep a doctor in this place or else turn the lights up." This was the first remark that Swarthout had ever addressed to me. We laughed to cover up our embarrassment.

When I came out, Swarthout was smoking in the middle of the bright bare room. Lights had been turned on and chairs had been piled on top of tables. Half a dozen Mexicans were sweeping straws and paper cups into trash cans. The transformation was appalling.

It was several minutes before my eyes became used to the bright whiteness. Then I saw Wade and Gerry between two artificial cactus plants. It was hideous. I wished we had gone sooner.

I said goodbye to Gerry Eaton in the purple glare of the neon Tower. He said something about writing when he got to his new assignment, but I wasn't listening. Then Wade Howell and I were alone in the taxi on our way to the Angus. We didn't say a word.

◆ ◆ ◆

In the middle of the night, I woke up in a dark room. My first thought was "How wonderful." Then I heard voices whispering at the door.

"I was only joking when I asked you to come up here. I was mad and I did it for spite."

"I'm not joking, Wade."

I recognized the little tug of sincerity in Gerry Eaton's tone. At one point I had been rather fond of this verbal frown, so to speak. Lord, how stale our love seemed now. And to think that we'd hardly finished with it. It was a perishable thing indeed.

"I'll bet you'd be wonderful in the sack...it would be such a romp...sentiment makes for such dreary love."

There followed a tender scuffle ending in a kiss.

"Love. I'm sick to death of love...if there is such a thing."

At that moment, I shared her feelings precisely. For a sweet fragrant breeze tempered my burning thoughts. A combination of objectivity and humor rescued me from self-pity. It was at this point that I decided it was high time that I entered the scene. I had a crazy notion that if I just sat up and giggled, I might salvage my wounded pride. But I decided that if I wasn't suffering from shock, I should be, and rest was my only salvation.

On the other hand, Gerry Eaton wasn't getting Wade's message at all.

"I like you for that," he said, rather too intensely.

"Go away, or you'll wake everyone up."

And he might at that.

"I don't care. Say, who's in there...another guy?"

All at once I shot out of bed and flipped the switch that sent us scampering like cockroaches for cover.

"Now it's two to one in favor of your leaving," I said.

"It was only a joke," he said.

"And I'm splitting with laughter. I never heard anything so funny. It's killing me. Now, go away so I can die in peace."

I thought I was being hysterical, but later Wade told me that my voice was calm and teasing. It struck her funny every time she mentioned it. Then I began to laugh. We laughed until we cried. And when we looked up, Gerry Eaton had gone away.

"I'm sorry for what I said before. I didn't mean it. I love it here." I knew she meant it.

We were so carried away with our giggling party that we couldn't bear to have it end. I found some rum and Coke in my mother's cabinet, and we drank until it was gone and so were we. Then we tumbled happily into bed and were real friends for the first time.

◆ TEN ◆

I woke up the next morning with a jolt. Slowly I became aware of a quiet confusion in the room, which at first I attributed to my unnatural position and the giddy distance to the ceiling. My usual position in bed was on my stomach, but since Wade Howell had moved in on me, I had learned to sleep huddled like an embryo facing the wall. Not so that last night.

It was the morning after the long day, and I never felt so bad in my life. There was a terrible pain in my back, my legs itched like sin, and it would take gallons of water to put out the fire in my throat. The champagne and rum had stopped bubbling and left me deflated. I didn't move. I just laid there in a heap looking at the two sweet glasses we had left on the window sill. They were covered with ants. I thought about water.

Then I realized that there were people in the room. Stealthy systematic people who were going about their business with all the quiet naturalness of termites. This was too much. But I couldn't bring myself to turn my head, much less make an effort to get out of bed, so I closed my eyes and stayed there in hateful

annoyance, hoping they would go away. I hadn't a shred of curiosity. The only thing that would save me from complete decay
was my desire for water. I decided in favor of decomposition.

I must have dozed off, for suddenly I sat up, startled. I couldn't
possibly have made such a courageous move in my former lethar-
gic condition. It had to come from being awakened from a brief
sound sleep.

Mrs. Howell and her daughter stopped packing to stare at me.
That is, Mrs. Howell stared. Wade sent me a meaningful message
of tender amusement. Despite her detachment, it annoyed me to
watch her playing the daughter.

Perhaps if I didn't speak, they would remain two cool beauties
in the hot Sunday sun. The cameo pink walls made a flattering
background for brunettes, all right. Then, first chance I had, I
would paint my room a deep blue and put some natural bamboo
blinds on the long windows.

But of course Mrs. Howell had no regard for privacy.

"Good morning," she said. "You're a sound sleeper."

I was in a foul mood, and this cozy greeting didn't improve
matters.

"Apparently, that's the only way I can keep my friends."

I punctuated the remark with a nasty stare in Wade's direction, but she was busy picking lint from last night's black linen
and chose not to notice. Anyway, it was a senseless thing to say
and had no connection with the source of irritation. After all,
we had laughed Gerry Eaton right out of our lives. Certainly
he could never show up again in any serious guise. Yet he had

played a very special part in those sweet holiday months—I will give him that much.

Now what bothered me was the clearheaded grace with which Wade Howell was packing up to leave without so much as a regretful backward glance. Perhaps there were certain advantages in having a ready-made life.

On the other hand, while Wade in her plush prison would be guarded on all sides, I could look forward to stretching out and languishing in the lush nights.

Getting out of bed and over to the washbasin was agony. If I hadn't felt that my personal habits were under the close scrutiny of two such fastidious creatures, I never would have made the effort. I managed to brush my teeth and throw water in my face before I looked in the mirror. Even so, I was disappointed. My face was pale and puffy and my hair made no sense at all. It would take all day to repair the damage, but with these two watching, I couldn't even begin. I never felt that my minute habits warranted even a limited audience. There was nothing to do but sit on the bed and wait.

It's funny, I thought, how impatient we are…even for unpleasantness.

I noticed that Wade Howell was more efficient than her mother. Mrs. Howell was inclined to be fluttery and hesitant, whereas Wade was all grace and economy of movement.

No wonder the men go wild over her, I thought. Those languorous gestures are wonderful in making love.

"Have you been spilling your vitamins again? There's a peculiar fishy smell in here."

These snappy little dismissals of all her daughter pretended to be made Eunice Estes Howell the mother. The powerful woman with the trivial emotions was unbeatable. I had a strong suspicion that Wade had always realized this and her defenses were more superficial gestures, the weak cries of the dying to show they had not turned to stone. At any rate, whatever Wade did was for the benefit of her mother. She played best to an audience of one.

Now, with her back to us, she was looking out the window. She was wearing a starched white piqué dress with a wide gold belt that I had often admired. Looking at her, I felt like a mess. I noticed she was smoking a cigarette, and I wondered if she had been out to breakfast. At least I should offer them coffee and rolls.

Turning slowly, and with a steady aim, she shot a cruel sure look through a circle of smoke and all but froze the air with her thin icy laugh. I thought she would never stop laughing, but when she did, she was in complete control.

"Mother, you're a scream," she said gaily. "You're so absolutely fouled up that you refuse to believe that I'm capable of performing any act on my own—good, bad, or indifferent." She flipped her cigarette through the window. "Which of us, may I ask, is going to sleep with Major Morris?"

The mother took this abuse as her due.

"Stop that!" she said mildly.

"Stop what?"

"That...that...filth."

"Here I am spilling out girlish confidences like you always want, and you all but put soap in my mouth. But that was an indelicate question. I forgot how you cringe before anything that has the slightest tinge of sensuality."

Beneath the surface gaiety of her daughter's tone, I detected the heavy burden of youthful honesty. She was itching for an all-out war, but this deceptive enemy was too old for honesty. She went right on folding lingerie for all she was worth. And I sat by, feeling sad without an ounce of pity for Mrs. Howell.

"By the way, did I tell you you look awful? And you should be getting enough sleep. But perhaps it's something else that's lacking, with the Colonel coming here for his—"

"Stop it!" And the mother slammed down the lid of the footlocker.

"She's very nice, you know. I really don't see why he ever left her. But then of course there is the money—those vague pots of gold that are scattered all over the world—doing no one any good...except you."

A quick look at the mother told me that she was not surprised. She was wearing a mask, all right, but a funny kind of mask that veiled the lower part of the face while the eyes revealed a wandering look of confusion. They dwelt on nothing. She had the faculty for looking at amazing things without being amazed.

But the pattern had been chosen eighteen years before, and except for minor alterations would be followed to the end. Wade Howell was the daughter.

The mother plunged herself into a complex check of duffel bags while the daughter played herself out in a softer key.

"You know, I'm perfectly happy here," she said. "I think the moldy, slightly used background is perfect for me—don't you, mother?"

"It's charming. The building is old, of course, but well cared for."

In a word, in a gesture, she shriveled whole worlds down to her level.

"Where is that vitamin bottle? I don't want any more of that smell around."

She tried to fasten the duffel bag, but her movements were weak and ineffectual. Hers was a victory of inner serenity. Or perhaps, more accurately, lack of emotion. Wade came to the rescue.

"I fed it to my last boyfriend as a parting gesture—he needed it, believe me."

She had unusual strength in her arms and hands. I realized for the first time that her delicate beauty hid a healthy body and an extraordinary vitality which she was driven to squander on restless wanderings and sporadic bursts of passion.

"Thank God I don't owe you any gratitude—then you'd be the healthy one. Isn't that right?"

I nodded, thinking the question was addressed to me.

The mother is nourished on overindulgence, not the child, I thought.

Shallow thoughts, no matter how trivial, usually hold up as remarkably sensible when pitted against the more profound reveries. At least, in everyday conversation.

I felt stupid in the face of Wade's question. I sensed in it an undertone of meaning that I was unable to grasp, and it infuriated me. I had long since reversed my opinion of Wade Howell. She was preoccupied, certainly, but never dull. But why did she have to become so subtly interesting in the morning when my senses were so blurred? My old feeling of inadequacy returned.

"I always tried to do what was best for you."

With this eternal parental excuse, Mrs. Howell slammed shut the last footlocker crammed with elegant simplicity.

"You always did what was best for you to do for me."

But Wade was no longer the intense fiery creature that I tried so hard not to envy. The fleeting desperate dream of passion on the run. She had taken a brief respite in the garden of her cloister, but she failed to scale the wall. Instead, she cut herself down to fit the pattern. She would marry Major Morris while on the other side of the wall her mother nodded in approval at the sounds of connubial love. And the pattern would be passed on.

I was somewhat embarrassed by this sensual display of emotions on a quiet Sunday morning. I despised myself for this narrow attitude. All the same, I had to escape. Coffee was the only answer. What was there in our national character that caused us to rely on an irritant to induce our most soothing moments? Yet it seemed natural enough.

"I'll make some coffee," I said at the door.

With an armful of clothes and all the toilet articles I could carry, I tore down the hall to my mother's apartment. Of course, she didn't approve of parading around the hall in a "lint catcher," but then she was in church.

My mother's bathroom was between a tiny kitchen and a tremendous bedroom. It was the largest room in the apartment and certainly the most elegant. In fact, I don't recall ever having seen a room with such natural charm and character. It reminded me of an old countess with adventure etched deeply into every line of her face. And why not? That bathroom boasted a background as sultry with intrigue as a Viennese spy. Of course, it hadn't always been a bathroom. First it had been an aquarium. Exotic fish once swam in the sunken marble tank where I was about to take my bath. And while I luxuriated in the bloodstained water, the high morning sun burst through the skylight, changing everything to jewelry.

"This wouldn't be such a bad place to die, after all," I thought.

I was thinking of the story of the first owner, who had stabbed his wife and thrown her to the fish. The Mexicans, according to Jess, will have no truck with faithlessness. Adultery is considered a private matter and is dealt with personally and on the spot. The man who fancied tropical fish was no exception.

I don't know what became of the fish. But it was later that a Mexican army officer commissioned an artist to carve the Aztec calendars that lined the walls. He wished to remind his mistress, as she lay in the sun, that her time belonged to him. So much for history.

I drained the water, dabbed my streak of sunlight with peroxide, and washed my head under the faucet while I soaked in clean water. A bath always seemed more worthwhile after wallowing in slime.

I dressed carefully in black and white linen. I had to, for although it had once been an expensive dress, I had bought it secondhand. It was rather threadbare, with a dignified "poor but proud" look about it. The deception pleased me as much as the soft leather belt. I would stay close to home, with a needle and thread handy. There was nothing to do but spread myself out with the Sunday paper and wait.

The *San Antonio Light* was black with war news. There was a victory in North Africa. Rommel had been flushed out and had slunk back to Germany. But of course this was what we had expected all along. It was simply a question of time. I tossed the papers aside. Newspapers irritated me. Their very dailiness and indiscriminating detail was as senseless as life itself, if not taken in hand.

Voices in the kitchen announced that church was over and what was left of the day was at the disposal of anyone fortunate enough not to have guests.

"That's a weight off my mind," my mother was saying. "They'll rent anything at the Shamrock—a half-dozen yards of cretonne and she thinks she has a three-dollar room."

"You don't know when you're well off. That child is a chore."

Lillie du Lac was merciless when it came to children. She had never had any of her own, and as far as she was concerned, anyone under fifteen should have been an abortion.

"It's the child I'm thinking of—she's entitled to a clean comfortable room."

At least half of this statement was true. My mother would

spend the afternoon scouring the room. Then her enthusiasm for arranging would take over with a vengeance. Furniture would be shifted from room to room. There would be endless grubbing around in the cellar after old draperies and half-used cans of paint. All in the name of that pitiful little girl. Well, we're all entitled to our prideful little deceits. Even wise old Lillie du Lac didn't mention Sergeant McCane.

I rushed into the kitchen to remind my mother not to change her clothes. I needn't have bothered. They were well aware that the Colonel's lady was at the Angus.

"There are limousines lined up from the Alamo to the Blue Room waiting to cart them off. Crowds are three abreast, expecting to see a full military parade."

Lillie du Lac was in rare form. Indeed, she had even gone to church with my mother knowing full well that there is no surer way to humble a rival than to stand before her in Sunday clothes with your Bible showing.

My mother carried this principle to extremes. With her, going to church was simply good business, one more weapon in the arsenal that kept her roomers in line. Not only that, she made use of the time by adding up her weekly receipts in a genteel little notebook with a gold pencil.

Then, too, it was an excuse to dress up. If my mother was content to sit in a prim corner in proper navy, not so Lillie du Lac. She was the picture of stunning opulence in beige shantung and a red hat the size of a wagon wheel. Naturally the cool austerity of my mother's church had no appeal for her friend. Christianity would have to wear a black cloak and go underground before it claimed Lillie's soul.

Lillie du Lac set a pot of coffee on the stove—the cue for the little whitewashed kitchen to come alive. My mother was of Scandinavian descent and coffee meant a meal. Rye bread and fish, homemade rolls and jam, and if I didn't distract her she'd start whipping up a cake.

"Where's Jess?" I asked.

"The preacher invited him and Mira for dinner."

"Oh, God!"

"Shame on you."

"All I said was 'Oh, God.' I thought it was quite appropriate."

"It wouldn't hurt you to go to church once in a while."

"I have my own religion that I make up as I go along—minus politics, war news, and cake sales."

My mother turned to her pickled herring. I had been with her long enough now to know that when we tangled with ideas it always ended on the same note: she was shocked by my self-indulgence. Yet I suspected that she agreed with me more than she cared to admit. She had certainly divorced herself from the well-ordered life of safe little friendships and congenial habits and treated herself to a mildly unconventional existence of her own choosing. She only pretended shock. She reacted the way she thought I expected her to react.

"My advice to you is to lay off the whiskey or you'll lose every tooth in your head—and that's not all you'll lose." This was Lillie du Lac.

I realized that all my pains in bathing and fussing with my clothes had not erased the dull signs of debauchery. If this was true, it was high time to enter a new stage. With my passion for cataloguing, I began dividing myself into periods. First, a poor but bright little half-orphan shuffled out among unappreciative relatives. Next, a serious half-grown Jane Davis slipping between the pages of her books to escape the inevitable. And finally a Jane Davis turned inside out...completely absorbed by the emotion of the moment. Was there a Jane Davis capable of permanent attachments? I wondered. But I was not at all certain that I was ready to enter this next stage.

At that time I wanted nothing more than to be free to wander in the hot suggestive streets. The very air intrigued me. It was in harmony with my sense, being neither harsh nor still and oppressive but rather elusive, like illicit lovers stirring in the dark. Time enough later on to leave myself wide open to the humdrum. I would guard my selfish private world for a while longer. Dissipation be damned.

There was a knock at the bathroom door. Wade Howell had not been at the Angus long enough to know her way around. When I opened the kitchen door, mother and daughter did an abrupt about-face in the dark hall and marched toward me with frilly giftwrapped boxes and foolish afternoon smiles. At first, it seemed the packages were so numerous as to cover the faces, and the smiles were a part of the jittery decor. Later, I realized that I had been deceived all around.

The hall was never dark in the daytime. How could it be? It

was blessed with that mysterious Spanish architectural phenom-enon which gave the impression of cool shaded shelter but never gloom. The two women seemed to have taken on the same style. Against the calm background, their finicky burdens had risen out of all proportion to their size and number. The mother was smiling vaguely, but the daughter had a terrible look of desper-ately controlled hysteria. I suspected that she had been laughing uncontrollably for some time.

"A little token of appreciation," Mrs. Howell was saying. "This has been an enlightening experience for Dede, to say the least."

"We've learned a few things ourselves."

I hadn't realized that Lillie du Lac was standing behind me. I introduced the Colonel's two wives.

"I've heard so much about you," Mrs. Howell said.

I stepped back and wondered what manner Lillie would adopt.

"I'll just bet you have," she said, in a particularly cloying tone.

Lillie du Lac could shout obscenities up three flights of stairs and over half a city block, but for this dainty affair, she had taken on the bitchy hiss of a tarnished Mardi Gras belle.

"Isn't it a wonderful surprise, Martha?"

While the rest of us were groping for words, my mother had done herself proud with a starched linen cloth, a bowl of fresh pineapple, and my grandmother's china cups.

"Of course, we hate to see you go." The words were for Wade, but Lillie's black eyes were all over Mrs. Howell, and her lower lip was stretched across her teeth in a gluttonous smile.

"But let's make it gay anyway. There are so few things to cele-brate these days."

Mrs. Howell had no subtle moods to fall back on, no flashes of irony, no quick smiles.

"This is just a little remembrance...nothing, really...to show our appreciation." She was poking the box at my mother, feeling around in desperation for a safety zone.

And Wade hung back—white against the white wall. How quickly she had slipped back into being her mother's daughter. One last painful lurch and she was lifeless again. But her eyes were on Lillie even as she handed me the box. How she must have envied this jubilant woman. But I couldn't be certain. Her eyes no longer cast their shadows. They were opaque.

Suddenly we were in an artificial garden. We were being buried in flowers. Flowers that reeked of artificial insemination: Tweed, Shocking, and Chanel No. 5. Pink, white, blue—pale albino flowers. The garden wall with its cracked, blistered, peeling surface was more alive than the flowers—or the people. Of course, I was the least alive of anyone.

Somewhere along the way, someone had taught me that it was proper to thank people for gifts. Smelling of Chanel No. 5, my mother had thanked Mrs. Howell for the pink, white, and blue lingerie. I hated gifts. They sent me spinning in confusion, groping for words of gratitude. And there were none that had either a sincere ring or a pleasant sound. Surely we were not meant to be placed in that awkward position.

"You must have coffee with us anyway," my mother said simply.

"But our cars are blocking the entrance."

"Bother the limousines," Lillie said. "The guests at the Angus won't mind. It will give them something to lean on." Mrs. Howell started for the door. "Don't worry. They wouldn't think of going inside. Most of them have cars of their own some place or other, or have had some time or other. It's only lately that they've taken to walking on their knees. It's for the war effort, you know."

Mrs. Howell made the fatal mistake of looking uncomfortable. When it came to belittling her opponents, Lillie made no mistakes.

"I know what you're thinking," Lillie went on, "and I could have spared you that little twitch of anxiety. We have no intention of upsetting your rubbish heap. We see all kinds of garbage around here, and it all begins to smell alike sooner or later. Now pull up a chair and have some coffee."

Mrs. Howell would not take the risk of being rude. She sat down. Between the strong coffee and the wild insinuations of Lillie du Lac, this would be a meal to remember. Indeed, from the way our guests ate, it looked as though they might intend it to be their last. They were all compliments. We settled back for a polite little coffee klatch.

"I don't want to appear inquisitive," Mrs. Howell said, "but where did you find that shantung?"

Lillie du Lac stood up and twirled around, holding out her arms in mock clumsiness.

"Pongee, it's called. A relic of the old Men Are Men days when men lived as long as their wives and didn't die off like poisoned rats, leaving rich young widows lurking in the shadows."

"At the time, I didn't realize—" Mrs. Howell sat back in sad confusion.

"Of course you didn't. The fact of the matter is that I had discarded the Colonel—for all practical purposes, that is—by the time you came along. So you really have nothing to blame yourself for. You can go right on being a couple of lovebirds."

Mrs. Howell sighed heavily, unable to work her way through Lillie's thick coat of irony.

"But to get back to the dress." Lillie made herself another herring sandwich. "And that's exactly what I said when I dragged it out of the trunk after all these years."

The refined tingling of china cups and the cozy talk of old trunks gave our little gathering a deceptive look of amiability as fragile as Lillie's little joke.

With a whiff of humor, Mrs. Howell might have blasted Lillie's game to bits. But like all dull people, she had no notion of fun. She knew as well as any of us that Lillie was wearing a new dress. Even the stupid have their limited powers of observation. And therein lies the trouble, for they can't conceive of intelligence beyond their own. To the great dumb Eunice, in her limited pink boundaries, the jest became a lie.

What puzzled me was the fact that Lillie went right on wasting her time. But perhaps we were the audience and Mrs. Howell was merely the foil. That was it, after all. Didn't the performance satisfy my small mean streak to a T? An outright execution would have been too much for me to stomach.

"Naturally it smelled moldy. That's what saved it. Otherwise I would have tossed it aside like any other old rag. But the terrible stink in my room made me stop and think."

Lillie moved closer to Mrs. Howell, who in turn moved closer to my mother.

"Don't worry, I soaked it in suds for days."

"I'm certain it's clean." Mrs. Howell was trying to be agreeable, but she only succeeded in being insipid, which irritated Lillie.

At this point it seemed to me that her tactics became more drastic. Up until then, she was simply showing off, turning cartwheels in the grass to show how well she could come out of an impossible situation.

"I can smell it from here," my mother said happily.

"Martha has a sensitive nose."

"I have to in this business. Many's the smoldering mattress I've tracked down in the middle of the night."

Suddenly Lillie's irritability exploded into viciousness.

"What kind of a stinker are you, Mrs. Howell?"

Good God, I thought, when is this crazed torturer going to allow her victim to come up for air?

"I'm pretty normal, I guess." The woman was really impossible. There was no getting to her at all.

"What a shame. You're missing so much. For instance, with a twist of the head like so—" Lillie bent her head down, "I get just a whiff of a long-lost scent. Ah, there we are. Why, it's the Colonel, of course. He's always smelled like that. Slightly moldy. Even lately I've noticed it."

Mrs. Howell turned white, but she said nothing. It wasn't shock, but confirmation of a suspicion.

"It comes from being stationed in the damp jungle all those

years before the war. But those were the days. They would have done wonders for you, my dear. Real character-builders." Lillie almost poked her long fingers into Mrs. Howell's open mouth. "There was some challenge to being in the army then. It was up to the women entirely. We clutched and clawed and tore our way to the top of first one little tropical outpost and then another. And the men sat and rotted. Now they're out fighting a war, or dreaming one at least, and once again they've become as virile as plebes." Toward the end there was a shrill note of lonely desperation that marred the tone. I had never seen Lillie du Lac look so tired.

Mrs. Howell stood up. "We didn't intend to stay so long."

Wade laid down her knife once again in obedient apathy. The mother noticed this and came to life once again. Against that maternal armor, the sharpest weapons are of no avail.

"Of course you didn't," my mother said, determined to the very end to steer us into polite inanity, "but we were such butter-fingers with the bows."

But of course Lillie du Lac was determined to have the last word, even though it was a little feeble.

"All you have to remember is to keep him away from the very young, the very beautiful, and the very passionate—but not necessarily in that order." And she gave Wade a knowing look.

Wade Howell seemed to cringe in the presence of Lillie du Lac, but I couldn't be certain, since it was less of a movement than a change of character. Her one gallant stand against Lillie had shown up her childish pretensions for what they were. Or so she thought. It would have pleased her to know that Lillie took her quite seriously. I must remember to tell her...sometime.

✦ ✦ ✦

My mother, Lillie du Lac, and I went up front to my room so we could watch the Howells leave. I noticed Wade's little wooden chest in the middle of the dusty dresser. My first thought was that she had intended to leave it. Perhaps she meant to use it as an excuse to return to the Angus. Knowing Wade as I did, I felt certain that the simple spontaneous act of returning for fun would be inconceivable to her. We each stood in a big window looking down at the two women and the two cars. I didn't mention the wooden chest.

We watched Wade Howell crawl into the second car and arrange herself in the tumble of luggage. Mrs. Howell stayed on the sidewalk to the very last, seeing about the other things. It was one o'clock, and the big thermometer on the Dairy Maid sign read 101 degrees. A real scorcher. I was sleepy.

Looking through windows had always made me sleepy. I thought vaguely of drowsy spring afternoons taunting me through classroom windows, of hot midday sun through stained-glass windows, and of teasing sunlight sifting through bamboo slats.

Just as Jess and Mira stopped by to say goodbye to Wade Howell, a squirrel on a wild venture after a pecan was run over by a Trailways bus. Only its tail rose out of the bloody heap, in lifelike defiance. Jess supported himself against the car as he gallantly gestured with his cane in another direction to draw their attention away from the nasty sight. A pathetic reminder of our insistent "chin up" attitude.

I wondered if Mira was experiencing the inevitable pangs of envy that every street urchin feels for the princess in the golden carriage. Probably not. Jess's unmistakable admiration gave her vulgarity the flattering look of natural gaiety struggling through sorrow. No doubt she realized her good fortune. Her meager desire would ensure that, just as her streak of innocence relied on a limited day-to-day fate to see her through.

"What will they do with the child?" Lillie du Lac said. She too had been watching Jess and Mira.

"Children belong with their mothers."

"Undoubtedly. Although at times I think it's slightly over-done." Lillie du Lac refused to be led away from the scene of her triumph.

"One thing at least, all that greedy love of hers has brought the Colonel around."

"In a small way, but even a little revenge is shamefully sweet."

At that point, I couldn't keep my eyes open. Pretending fascination with the little wooden chest, I sat on the bed, while my mother and Lillie du Lac went scraping and digging through the soggy marshes and infected tropics of the past. I fell asleep still wearing the dress I had pressed so carefully.

Coming out of a brief sound sleep, I found myself enmeshed in ghosts. Soft gentle ghosts. Hard sharp little ghosts. Miniature ghosts. And inescapable entangling ghosts.

Keepsakes. The collection was rather ordinary, I thought. And

I despised my cheap freshman cynicism. Nonetheless, it was the usual lock of hair, pressed flowers, and seashells. I picked a small envelope out of the clutter. The note read:

My Dear Friend,

I will not be back to claim these little mementoes. Whether you keep them or not is all the same to me. My only regret is that I did not learn to know you better. Then I would be able to foresee what you would do. Do not forget the note I gave you last night. There again I cannot anticipate your decision.

Fondly,

Wade Howell

I made a rush for the laundry bag and started digging around for my pocketbook.

That old white jersey would look stunning with the frayed pockets bound in black velvet, I thought.

The note was covered with pencil shavings and smeared with pancake makeup, but it was readable.

Dear Jane,

I have a date to meet a darling lieutenant at 2:15 Sunday in front of the Alamo. We had planned to take the sightseeing tour that leaves at 2:30. Since I told him not to wait if I wasn't there, I am certain he will go on without me. He is quite the tourist. Takes a camera wherever he goes. I know this makes him sound drippy, but it is only that he is so young and needs someone to jolt him out of his stupor. Of course, combat duty would help, but he is an instructor at Randolph, and I doubt if he will ever see much action unless someone steps in.

Tomorrow is my birthday, and I know that Mother will drag me off to enjoy the comforts of home among other things. I simply don't have what it takes to go off on my own.

The point is this: Why let a perfectly adorable lieutenant go to waste? And you've never seen the Mission San Francisco de la Espada. It's been fun.

Fondly,

Wade Howell

It was two o'clock. I stuffed the white jersey back into the laundry bag.

Whatever gave me the idea that I am clever? I thought. White wool in this climate!

Anyway, black and white was not my style. It took a beauty like Wade to carry that off without looking like an usherette. My monotones needed hot pink or Mexican yellow.

Suddenly, in front of the Menger Hotel, I had an absurd feeling of shyness, and for a moment I could hardly bear to be alive. It was ridiculous, of course. Up until then, I had been carried along through the blistering sun by vague thoughts of changing jobs and settling down to a stiff dose of Chaucer.

I paused before the shop where we had met many times. A dozen familiar pouting faces looked back at me from an old silver chafing dish, and I felt a sweet thrill of loneliness. I missed Wade Howell.

I turned toward the Alamo, brilliant in the fiery sun. There was the lieutenant. Wade was right. I started to run. Then I slowed down, realizing I had a whole day in the sun, and that at night a cool breeze would blow in through my window.

Streetwise

CHAR MILLER

The Duchess of Angus is driven by a kind of kinetic energy that animates its central characters' actions, shapes its readers' affective responses, and creates a dynamic mapping of 1940s San Antonio, a city then buffeted by a series of social and economic forces that World War II unleashed.

Surely that may account for why Margaret Brown Kilik opens the novel with a rush, a welter of words, thoughts, asides, and emotions. Some expressed, others not. The novel's cinematic quick cuts from one site to another—the imposing post office in San Antonio's central core; the clean, well-lit Manhattan Cafe, which "had nothing to offer but sanitation"; the River Walk stairway that was "wide and cool and smelled of dampness"—are of a piece with the protagonist's fraught sense of herself. An early and unsettling exchange with an overeager, blundering suitor leaves Jane Davis shaken by "deep personal outrage. It was as though someone were trampling on my shadow. Or perhaps I was the shadow." As disorienting as this reflection is for her, and even as it sets up one of the novel's throughlines—that Jane, however partially, will over time confront her propensity to live in the shade of others—it contributes to the reader's confusion. We have been dropped into the story mid-flow, without a map or compass, without referent or bearing. Where are we?

This haunting sense of being out of place and time is one way that Kilik, who lived in San Antonio during the 1940s, evokes the churning, disruptive impact of the city's wartime boom. And boom it was, too, especially when compared to the previous decade, in which the Great Depression had flattened the local economy with the steep and slashing decline in military spending at the city's five major forts and airfields and the near-total collapse of a once-vibrant tourist trade. The Depression also shut off what hitherto had been a substantial inflow of new residents— between 1910 and 1930 San Antonio had grown on average more than 60 percent a decade. Across the 1930s, by contrast, it grew a paltry 9 percent. Bearing the downturn's brunt was the large and already poor population of Mexican Americans and Mexican immigrants, many of whom were segregated in squalid conditions on the west side—a grinding immiseration that *Duchess of Angus* barely notices.[3] When the narrative does mention the city's Hispanic community, it offers up its victims as a dash of color (in every sense), foils in the otherwise all-white world through which its more privileged Anglo characters move.[4]

It was not until the late 1930s that economic conditions in San Antonio improved.[5] Spurred by Japanese aggression in China and Southeast Asia and the rise of the Axis powers in Europe, and following the 1936 election, the Roosevelt administration and Congress began to shift federal dollars away from social services and to the War Department. San Antonio was among the beneficiaries of this reversal of fortune: ultimately more than $1 billion would be channeled to the city to fund the wartime missions of Fort Sam Houston and Randolph, Kelly, Brooks, and Lackland Air Fields, as well as numerous related installations. Hundreds of thousands of soldiers, aviators, and health care workers were trained in and around the now jammed town. Thousands of civilian defense workers were hired to construct barracks, runways, and base extensions, to repair aircraft, and to feed and clothe the troops. The rapid inflow of fiscal and human resources flipped the Depression-era challenges on their head: once there were few, if any, jobs in San Antonio, now there was a surfeit; once there was little disposable income, now there seemed an endless stream of cash; once bankrupt homeowners lost the roof over their heads, now the city was beset with a severe housing shortage.[6] World War II, and more precisely the massive federal investment in it, brought life-changing prosperity to the Alamo City.

Kilik makes considerable use of the city's uptick. Its swelling growth (in 1940 the census tallied 253,854 residents; in 1950 there were 408,442), and its frenetic pace and disjointed beat, drive *The Duchess of Angus*'s narrative tempo. The "hot Saturday night crowds had kept the sidewalks from cooling off," Jane observes one sweltering eve. Her favorite haunts sizzle: Frenchie's

Black Cat Café was "a clattering twenty-four-hour slop house"; at the Tower Club, shadowy and enormous, "the possibility for amusement seemed infinite against the cheap glow of pink and green and blue lights." Each night the bars, clubs, and dance halls teemed with recruits—eager, yearning, leering. Pilots had a special allure. "Dating an aviation cadet was a rather breathless experience," Jane declares, "for they had a wonderfully frantic way about them, as though they were running for a troop train."

In jumped-up San Antonio, it was tough to get around. Traffic seemed to grind to a halt. Hailing a cab proved a chore; like sardines, "young army wives and their unhealthy babies and old Mexican women in black shawls on unhealthy religious pilgrimages" packed the Greyhound bus depot. Pedestrians were right to be skittish: it took "luck and perseverance" to cross the "crazy five-point intersection" of Losoya and Commerce, which "was no worse than dozens of legalized death traps where madmen went around on wheels." There was even a pulse to Jane's absenteeism at work, which her employer, Joske's department store, took in stride, accepting "my spasmodic illnesses as a symbol of the times."

Despite San Antonio's edgy explosiveness, notwithstanding its hectic hum, the peripatetic Jane sticks pretty close to home, tightly bound in a city that seems without limit. Her epicenter is the Angus Hotel on South Alamo, from which she can gaze on the "CCM Bar, the Riverside Café, the Saddle Club, the haunts of shabby lushes," all sited a "city block from daytime respectability." Her daily round does not extend much beyond this locale.

It would have taken her only a couple of minutes to walk north to her job at Joske's, its prominent facade commanding the corner of Alamo and Commerce. Where Jane eats and shops, where she dances, dreams, and drinks, where she is almost raped and where she tries to lose her virginity—this all occurs in a narrow segment of the central business district framed by Alamo Plaza on the east, Houston Street on the north, and perhaps, though unmentioned, Saint Mary's Street to the west. She never hops on any of San Antonio's nineteen streetcar lines, for example, which would have carried her to nearly every corner of the city's thirty-six-square-mile expanse. The sole exceptions to this cramped range are Jane's bus trip to Fort Sam Houston, a four-mile jaunt to the northeast, and a wild inebriated taxi ride to Kelly Field. So while she inhabits a boisterous, war-fevered mid-twentieth-century city, her experience of it is insular and insulated; her comfort zone is relegated to a portion of its eighteenth-century Spanish colonial grid.

Until, that is, the novel's final pages. The setup involves a handoff of a "darling lieutenant" that Jane's friend and roommate Wade Howell had arranged to meet in Alamo Plaza to catch a bus for a day of sightseeing. Because "tomorrow is my birthday, and I know that Mother will drag me off to enjoy the comforts of home among other things," Wade urges Jane to sub in for her. "He is quite the tourist. Takes a camera wherever he goes. I know this makes him sound drippy, but it is only that he is so young and needs someone to jolt him out of his stupor." Implied too is the idea that Jane needs to break out: "Why let

244 • CHAR MILLER

a perfectly adorable lieutenant go to waste? And you've never seen the Mission San Francisco de la Espada."[7] At the appointed hour on a Sunday afternoon, Jane hesitates: "Suddenly, in front of the Menger Hotel, I had an absurd feeling of shyness, and for a moment I could hardly bear to be alive."

But she pushes ahead, rounding the corner into Alamo Plaza, "brilliant in the fiery sun," and spots her blind date. "Wade was right. I started to run. Then I slowed down, realizing I had a whole day in the sun, and that at night a cool breeze would blow in through my window."

Jane's horizons are widening. She is gaining ground.

Beyond Adobe Walls

Anglo Perceptions and the Social Realities of San Antonio's "Mexican Quarter"

LAURA HERNÁNDEZ-EHRISMAN

One difficult truth of living in a profoundly unequal society is that people can live in close proximity to one another and yet know very little about each other's lives. People who are divided by race, class, or gender often do not see or understand one another's perspectives, even when they inhabit the same spaces on a daily basis. At the same time, people of privilege often have a strong desire to know about marginalized communities, and so they spend a great deal of time peering into the physical and social worlds of the "other." What they perceive, however, is more often a projection of their own fears and desires.

I agree with Jenny Davidson when she notes that Margaret Kilik's novel is a valuable time capsule for understanding San Antonio during the World War II era. The novel offers insights into how Anglo-Americans perceived Mexican Americans in the early and mid-twentieth century. In Kilik's novel, the protagonist Jane Davis is constantly aware of "Mexicans" who stand on streets and along the river, work in the restaurants where she eats, and clean the rooms of her mother's hotel. Most of them are unnamed, part of the scenic background of her time in the city. But she notices them, remarks on their presence, and is drawn to the "Mexican Quarter" for its "comforting yet melancholy sense of timelessness." Using racialized stereotypes, she describes the Mexicans' "sad gaiety" as they "mentally threw up their hands and gave up the exhausting struggle of trying to imitate their conquerors." She offers the question of "just who had conquered whom" as an expression of her longing for something different.

Kilik is speaking to what some white Americans were drawn to in San Antonio, something that made the city distinct from many other American places. In the early twentieth century in particular, many white American tourists were looking for authenticity, and they were seeking it in the Southwest, America's "orient." This was a time when recovering a distinctly American past became increasingly important to Americans.[8] The character of Jane Davis echoes the thoughts of many Americans who responded to the displacements of modernity by looking for a rootedness in the Native American and Mexican cultures of the southwestern United States, which was imagined as a place to find a preindustrial, unchanging simplicity and thus an antidote to modern life.[9]

Yet Kilik's novel also reveals a city in the midst of significant historical transformations and focuses on characters who are in transition, pulled by the forces of war. The entire novel is framed by Jane's experiences dating servicemen temporarily stationed at Fort Sam Houston or Randolph Air Force Base. Jane, returning from college, is not ready to live a settled life. Perhaps this is why she embraces what she calls the "carnival spirit of the city." As she and her companion Wade Howell explore the city's nightlife, they are engaging in what they know is a temporary escape from the lives they will eventually assume. The "Mexican Quarter," in particular, seems to be a space for these young women to explore their sexuality. Though Jane is not as promiscuous as her friend Wade, she joins her hunt for *cascarones* (what she calls confetti eggs), which seem to become a symbol of her growing sexual desires. After she buys the eggs, she tucks two of them in her bra; an egg breaks as she is kissed by a cadet and the confetti trails from a hole in her dress all evening as she meets with various other servicemen. Wade goes much further than this, and exchanges sex for food with a Mexican man. Kilik's novel is just one of many examples of the orientalizing of Mexican culture in the United States, representing the Mexican Quarter as a place of less restricted sexuality and vice.

What is particularly interesting about Jane's perspective is that she is also aware of the precariousness of her own status. Unlike Wade, she is not part of a prominent military family. Her mother was once a maid and then owns a series of rundown hotels. They are relatively stable because of the war, but Jane remembers the hard times of the Depression. She recognizes how servicemen may condescendingly view her "bohemian" lifestyle. She also seems to resent the Howells' wealth. There is an interesting parallel between the way Wade intrudes on Jane's hotel in order to experience greater freedom and the way Jane immerses herself in the Mexican Quarter. But Jane seems to realize that she has more to lose. Unlike her brother Jess, who describes a brief relationship with a Mexican woman when he traveled to Mexico, Jane does not seem to have the same freedom (or maybe even the desire) to pursue such a relationship. Instead she prefers to express an attachment to adobe walls and other reminders of the city's Spanish heritage. Her narrative reinforces the contradictory attitudes of many Anglo-Americans toward Mexicans—a desire to consume Mexican culture coexisting with a desire to distance themselves from Mexican people.

San Antonio, founded in 1773 on the edges of New Spain, has always been shaped by this heritage as part of Spanish Texas and Mexico. Tourists and city boosters have romanticized this part of the city's past, writing with "imperialist nostalgia" about the place that had been transformed by Americanization and manifest destiny.[10] After the founding of the Republic of Texas in 1835, as Richard Garcia notes, San Antonio and its Mexican population had "a symbiotic relationship," a "curious strain of Texas pride and arrogance complemented by a growing hatred of Mexicans, even while the city retained, ironically, a pride in its Spanish heritage."[11] In the remaining decades of the nineteenth century, Mexican Americans lost much of their power and status in the city. They were pushed off their lands, killed by Anglo mobs, barred from Anglo public establishments, and segregated in schools and neighborhoods.

In American society, Mexicans were viewed as other though at times also as white, and whiteness was linked to the rights of full citizenship.[12] This could be traced from the earliest laws defining national citizenship, outlined in the Naturalization Act of 1790, a law that allowed citizenship only for free white persons. Mexican Americans were discriminated against because they were never considered fully white. On the other hand, they were also "spared the full impact of racial discrimination because of their Spanish descent."[13] This contradiction was reinforced by the "Spanish fantasy" promoted throughout the Southwest—encouraging an interest in old Spanish buildings and traditions but also defining contemporary Mexican Americans as racial others.

Anti-Mexican violence would continue in the first four decades of the twentieth century, even as San Antonio was becoming a modern city and, once again, more Mexican. During the early twentieth century the city was referred to as the "financial, educational, cultural, and recreational capital of South Texas as well as a wholesale distributing and retail trading center."[14] The people who labored to build San Antonio were predominantly Mexican Americans. They worked in railroad yards, packing plants, military bases, garment factories, service establishments, and the retail trade.[15] During those decades newly arrived Mexican migrants joined older generations of Tejanos, and the city's Mexican American population increased from 13,722 in 1900 to 103,000 in 1940 (from 25.7 to 46.3 percent of the population).[16] These migrants were fleeing poverty and the chaos of the Mexican Revolution, but they were also finding economic opportunities in a city and region that needed their labor. At the beginning of World War II, Mexican Americans made up about half of San Antonio's population.

San Antonio had been divided into ethnic quadrants since the 1850s, and each of these ethnic "towns" had their distinct social realities.[17] While some Tejano families from the nineteenth century had integrated into the Anglo population, most Mexican Americans were segregated in the city's west side (the Latin or Mexican Quarter). Mexican Americans were restricted from buying homes outside the west side, unless they claimed to be Spanish.[18] This side of town was characterized by poverty and high rates of tuberculosis, a lack of public facilities, and the second highest death rate of the five largest cities in Texas. In 1939 the west side was described as "one of the most extensive slum areas anywhere in the world."[19]

As the Great Depression hit, anti-Mexican sentiment once again intensified. Congress debated new laws restricting immigration, and "literacy, hygiene, and financial tests were enforced with renewed vigor to keep Mexicans out."[20] In 1929, for the first time, crossing the border without proper documents became punishable as a federal crime.[21] Then the US government "turned to administrative tools such as deportation to control the Mexican population. Mexicans accounted for more than 46 percent of all those deported between 1930 and 1939, though they represented only 1 percent of the US population."[22] San

Antonio was already known as the gateway to Mexico; half of the
22,952 Mexicans who were deported from Texas came through
the San Antonio immigration and naturalization service district.

Mexican Americans' racial categorization was also redefined
during this time. In the list of possible "races" in the 1930 government census, the category of Mexican was added for the first
and only time in US history. This was already a pejorative term
used by Anglos, which is why many Mexican Americans tended
to call themselves Latin Americans.

Despite these stark facts, it is critical to note that, for Mexican
Americans, San Antonio was an important cultural capital. Like
Los Angeles and El Paso, San Antonio had vibrant cultural in-
stitutions—including a prominent Spanish-language daily newspaper and radio station. The Mexican American community's
social and cultural life centered around Haymarket, Milam, and
Alamo Plazas. The plazas were spaces to enjoy mariachi music
and Spanish conversation, with savory smells of the chili stands,
filled with tacos, tamales, enchiladas, and other Mexican cuisine.
Mexican Americans could also visit the Majestic or Empire the-
aters for movies and variety shows in English or Spanish. On the
city's west side there was an "undercurrent of Mexican spirit and
tradition," which was revived continually by new immigrants.[23]

This community was also politically engaged. In 1929 the
League of United Latin American Citizens (LULAC) was
founded in the city, and the organization would become one
of the country's most important civil rights organizations for
Latinos. Its foundation reflected a small but growing Mexican

American middle class, made up of small-business owners, professionals, and skilled workers. Mexican American working-class organizations also advocated for better working wages and working conditions in the early twentieth century, and this intensified during the Depression. In 1934 five thousand workers from the independent unions in the city's pecan sheller factories went on strike, followed a month later by bakers, and then by cigar workers in 1935. Then pecan sheller workers organized once again with a new union led by Emma Tenayuca.[24] Nearly twelve thousand workers, mainly Mexican American women, led a three-month strike in 1938. All of these events demonstrate a politically engaged Mexican American community that defied derogatory stereotypes of laziness or defeatism.

One would not expect to see the complexity of this Mexican American social world in Margaret Brown Kilik's novel, yet there are interesting hints of some changes in her brief story "Forfeit." This story parallels Kilik's novel in several ways, with a similar protagonist, but the main character's rival here is a Mexican American maid, Rita, who has become "one of the family." The protagonist, seeking revenge on her cousin Edward, sets him up with Rita with the expectation that their relationship will not be accepted by the family: "They had no future. Rita was accepted as one of the family as long as she was the maid. As long as the peasant remains the peasant, he is approved....But when the prince wishes to marry the scullery maid—that is another matter. Distinguished, dignified Edward Lennet and beautiful Rita Lopez were about to be defeated." She is disappointed, however, when she learns that the engagement is welcomed by the family, and Rita, it appears, will truly become a social equal in the household.

Does this brief episode hint at larger social changes, both in San Antonio and the country? World War II certainly increased employment opportunities for Mexican Americans in shipyards, airship factories, the oil industry, the mines, the munition factories, and numerous military and naval installations—particularly for skilled positions.[25] It is also important to note that LULAC and other civil rights organizations advocated for the elimination of the "Mexican" census category, and so once again most Mexican Americans would be counted as white. As a result of these changes, Mexican Americans "experienced the exhilaration of a new sense of economic and social possibility, personal hope, and self-development."[26] And more than 400,000 Mexican American veterans who returned home would sense these possibilities as they pressed for "social acceptance, civil and political rights, decent education, and expanded economic opportunities." They demanded "citizenship, in its fullest sense."[27]

In *San Antonio: A Historical and Pictorial Guide* (which was published in 1959, around the same time this novel was completed), Charles Ramsdell included a section about the "Mexican Town" but noted that this was a neighborhood in the midst of transformation. Haymarket Plaza still existed, but it was "covered over with a shed, not the lively place it used to be." And Produce Row was still lined with small restaurants and shops, but "the Mexican town, nowadays, is hard to find because it has grown so immense." In the paragraph that follows, Ramsdell includes some interesting political commentary. He says (note the passive voice) that "it was noticed, with some shock, that candidates with Spanish names almost invariably got elected when they ran for office" and parenthetically notes that "a Latin American is a Mexican with a poll tax, they quip."[28] For Ramsdell this "was a surprising turn, for until very recently Mexicans seldom bothered to vote unless they or someone in their family had a job at stake." Following this, he gives an account of how World War II offered Mexican American families opportunities to earn decent wages, buy a car and a house, and become a part of the middle class.[29]

Ramsdell described the ways that World War II had helped usher in important changes for Mexican Americans. Yet his political commentary reveals significant prejudices. He repeats the myth of the "sleeping giant"—the idea that Mexican Americans are politically apathetic—and it is difficult to ignore the hurtful quip about Latin Americans as "Mexicans with a poll tax." Ramsdell seems to mock Mexican Americans' efforts to distance themselves from a word that Anglos had made into an insult, nor does he acknowledge that the poll tax was one of many deliberate efforts to hinder the voting rights of Mexican and African Americans (it wasn't abolished until 1966). Ramsdell's remarks also reveal his expectation that his guidebook will be read by a predominantly Anglo audience, and that these prejudices are shared widely enough that readers will not reject them.

I highlight this text to demonstrate both what had changed and what had not in the postwar era. The stubborn resilience of racism is troubling but not that surprising. Indeed, at the moment of this novel's publication, we hear much of the same derogatory language. President Donald Trump's inflammatory rhetoric—calling Mexicans drug dealers, criminals, and rapists, charges he repeated during and after the 2016 election—was an unfortunately successful tactic in rallying some of his supporters; it was also a reminder that we are not living in a postracial society.

What value, then, is there in reading a novel that holds so many of these painfully familiar prejudices? Perhaps this story will help us become more aware of racism's long history and how cruel stereotypes were widely circulated in both fiction and nonfiction. As we cringe at the dated language in these works, we may become more critical of the contemporary prejudices that distance us from one another today.

Perhaps this is also a reminder to be more curious and open to the complexity of other peoples' lives, and to remember that understanding culture is about more than consuming great food and music.

ACKNOWLEDGMENTS

I would especially like to thank Della Daniels and family for the time they spent talking with me about Margaret and Agnes. Della's daughter, Jennifer Denslow, hosted lunch for us in her San Antonio home, and her son Tim Daniels and his wife, Kellie Sue, contributed a great deal to the conversation.

Particular thanks are due to Jon Kilik and Gretchen Kraus for their work putting together a record of Margaret's work as a gallerist, and for their willingness to share information and digital photographs. I would also like to thank Jon for handling contract-related paperwork in his role as executor of the Eugene L. Kilik estate. Mimi Lipson typed the manuscript, gave it a light initial copyedit, and encouraged me in my belief that the novel should be published.

Sara Mouch, university archivist at the University of Toledo, found Margaret's yearbook pages and clarified my understanding of the university environment during Margaret's years there as an undergraduate, and Colleen Hoelscher, special collections librarian at Trinity University, was quick to welcome the idea that Margaret's literary papers should be deposited in the university archives. Marguerite Avery and her colleagues at Trinity University Press have been wonderful to work with, and Laura

Hernández-Ehrisman and Char Miller's contributions are immensely valuable. Copyeditor Emily Jerman Schuster caught errors and made suggestions that have improved the novel in several significant ways.

Most of my own work on the project took place during a year I spent at Columbia University's Institute for Ideas and Imagination, and I am grateful to both the university and the institute for that support. Special thanks to the institute's library team, Grant Rosenberg, Meredith Levin, and Zack Lane and his colleagues in Butler Library's delivery services.

I am especially grateful to my mother, Caroline Davidson, for bringing me into the Kilik fold and for helping me contact Texas relatives, as well as to our dear friend Darren McCormack for taking such good care of Gene during the last year of his life. My only regret is that neither Gene nor his and Margaret's son, Jim, lived to see this book come to fruition. I dedicate the project to their memory, and to Margaret's.

NOTES

THE DISCOVER

1. "In Dialogue: Eugene Kilik and Gretchen Kraus," in *Margaret Kilik: The Key Gallery* (Beacon, NY: Space Sisters Press, 2018), 21.

2. "In Dialogue," in *Margaret Kilik: The Key Gallery*, 22.

STREETWISE

3. See Char Miller, *Deep in the Heart of San Antonio: Land and Life in South Texas* (San Antonio: Trinity University Press, 2004), 117–27, for a discussion of life on the city's west side.

4. Laura Hernández-Ehrisman's essay provides a more complete analysis of the novel's racial blinders.

5. See Char Miller, *San Antonio: A Tricentennial History* (Austin: Texas State Historical Association, 2018), 104–30, for an extended analysis of the city's transition out of the Great Depression and into the wartime economy.

6. My father, Frank L. Miller III, experienced that housing crunch when he arrived at Kelly Air Field for his pilot training, before shipping out to the China-Burma-India theater, where he flew C-47s over the Himalayas to ferry troops into conflict and the wounded back to hospitals in India; on one such flight, he met my mother, Helen Hartnett, a flight nurse. However structured his daytime hours might have been, apparently he did not sleep on the overwhelmingly jammed base: virtually every letter he wrote to his parents and first wife in Chattanooga, Tennessee, bore a different return address in San Antonio, as he sought housing wherever he could.

7. Mission San Francisco de la Espada is located ten miles south of Alamo Plaza.

BEYOND ADOBE WALLS

8. John Bodnar discusses this in *Remaking America: Public Memory, Commemoration, and Patriotism in the Twentieth Century* (Princeton, NJ: Princeton University Press, 1992).

9. Laura Hernández-Ehrisman, *Inventing the Fiesta City: Heritage and Carnival in San Antonio* (Albuquerque: University of New Mexico Press, 2008), 77.

10. Hernández-Ehrisman, *Inventing the Fiesta City*, 75.

11. Richard Garcia, *Rise of the Mexican American Middle Class: San Antonio, 1929–1941* (College Station: Texas A&M University Press, 1991), 16.

12. Melita M. Garza, *They Came to Toil: Newspaper Representations of Mexicans and Immigrants in the Great Depression* (Austin: University of Texas Press, 2018), 8.

13. Martha Menchaca, *Recovering History, Constructing Race: The Indian, Black, and White Roots of Mexican Americans* (Austin: University of Texas Press, 2001).

14. Lewis Simpson, "The Southern Recovery of Memory and History," *Sewanee Review* 82 (1974): 5.

15. San Antonio Public Service Company, Economic and Industrial Survey, 1942, 6, 31, 32. Referenced in Garcia, *Rise of the Mexican American Middle Class*, 29.

16. Ibid.

17. Garcia, *Rise of the Mexican American Middle Class*, 24; Hernández-Ehrisman, *Inventing the Fiesta City*, 57.

18. Hernández-Ehrisman, *Inventing the Fiesta City*, 79.

19. Garcia, *Rise of the Mexican American Middle Class*, 38.

20. Garza, *They Came to Toil*, 3.

21. Mae Ngai, *Impossible Subjects: Illegal Aliens and the Making of Modern America* (Princeton, NJ: Princeton University Press, 2004), 60.

22. Francisco E. Balderrama and Raymond Rodríguez, *Decade of Betrayal: Mexican Repatriation in the 1930s*, rev. ed. (Albuquerque: University of New Mexico Press, 2006), 67.

23. Garcia, *Rise of the Mexican American Middle Class*, 78–79.

24. Ibid., 62–63.

25. Carlos Castañeda, quoted in Garcia, *Rise of the Mexican American Middle Class*, 302.

26. Ibid.

27. Feliciano Rivera, quoted in Garcia, *Rise of the Mexican American Middle Class*, 303.

28. Charles Ramsdell, *San Antonio: A Historical and Pictorial Guide* (Austin: University of Texas Press, 1959), 163.

29. Ibid., 164.

MARGARET BROWN KILIK was raised by a single mother, and they moved frequently throughout the country during her childhood. Kilik graduated from the University of Toledo with a degree in English and subsequently lived in San Antonio, where she renewed a relationship with Eugene Kilik, whom she married. They spent the majority of their lives in New Jersey and New York City, where Kilik established and ran the Key Gallery in Soho. She was a collage artist and writer, and her only novel, *The Duchess of Angus*, written in the early 1950s, was discovered after her death. She died in New Jersey in 2001.

JENNY DAVIDSON is a professor of English and comparative literature at Columbia University and the author of four novels and four books of literary criticism. She was a fellow of the inaugural cohort at the Columbia Institute for Ideas and Imagination in 2018–19, and she is the recipient of a Guggenheim fellowship and Columbia University's Lenfest Distinguished Faculty and Mark Van Doren Teaching Awards, among other honors.

LAURA HERNÁNDEZ-EHRISMAN is an associate professor and chair of the Department of University Studies at St. Edwards University in Austin, Texas, and the author of *Inventing the Fiesta City: Heritage and Carnival in San Antonio*.

CHAR MILLER is the W. M. Keck Professor of Environmental Analysis at Pomona College and a former professor of history at Trinity University. He is the author of *Deep in the Heart of Texas: Land and Life in South Texas*, *Not So Golden State: Sustainability vs. the California Dream*, and *On the Edge: Water, Immigration, and Politics in the Southwest*, all from Trinity University Press.